JAWS OF DEATH

Boxer looked toward the rock. The shark's dorsal fin was now cleaving the water between the rock and the woman in the water.

"Ease up," he yelled back to the man at the outboard. "Ease up!" And he made a slicing motion across his throat.

"He'll circle around a couple of times," Boxer said, pointing to the dorsal fin. "You ease the boat toward the woman, and get her aboard."

"What the hell are you going to do?" the man asked.

"Watch," Boxer said, picking up a long knife that was used for flaying fish, then turning toward the bow.

"Come back," the man shouted.

Boxer didn't answer. The dorsal fin was less than ten yards away. He took a deep breath, executed a surface dive, and saw the gray, bullet shape streaking toward him.

The shark's mouth was already open . . .

ZEBRA BOOKS
KENSINGTON PUBLISHING CORP.

ZEBRA BOOKS

are published by

Kensington Publishing Corp.
475 Park Avenue South
New York, NY 10016

First printing: December, 1990

Printed in the United States of America

1

Boxer knew the meeting was important, because it was scheduled for 0730 in the office of the new director of the CIA, Mr. William C. Kahn . . . a new president always meant new men in key positions. It was part and parcel of the political payoff system of government. Even the CNO, Admiral Samuel Pierce, was new, and though he was a member of the Joint Chiefs of Staff, he wasn't the top man. That position was held by General Todd E. Yost, the first black man to hold the post.

Boxer, in uniform, flew down to Langley from New York on a navy helo, and arrived in Kahn's office ten minutes before the meeting.

Yost was already there, and when Boxer arrived, he looked up from the papers on his lap, and over the tops of his half glasses, nodded, and said, "You're Admiral Boxer, aren't you?"

"Yes, sir," Boxer answered.

Yost nodded, and went back to reading the papers on his lap.

Boxer settled in one of the empty chairs in front of

Kahn's desk, and concentrated on the tinted window behind it. The window looked out on a bare winter landscape, which was still spotted with patches of snow from a storm that swept up the Atlantic coast from Cape Hatteras, bringing more than eight inches of snow to the New York area, before heading into New England.

The door opened as Admiral Pierce entered.

Boxer stood up and saluted him.

Pierce returned the salute, and said, "It's cold out there . . . I'm told that more snow is on the way . . . This time from the west."

Both men sat down, then Boxer said, "I can't say that I like snow very much, even to look at." He was thinking of his various experiences in the Arctic and Antarctica.

Pierce didn't answer, and he and Yost nodded to each other, but didn't speak.

The door opened again, and Kahn entered. "Coffee and rolls will be here shortly," he said, in a booming voice that matched his frame. He looked like a linebacker; he even had the bull neck of a linebacker.

The three officers stood up.

"Well, Admiral," he exclaimed, walking directly toward Boxer, "I've wanted to meet you for a long while."

He offered his hand.

And Boxer shook it . . . the man had a grip like a linebacker too.

"Gentlemen, you'll be much more comfortable seated around the coffee table than arranged in front of my desk," Pierce said.

Yost and Pierce shared a small brown leather couch.

Boxer settled onto a white leather wing chair, and Kahn sat on a large tan leather easy chair.

Almost as soon as they were seated, there were several soft raps on the door, which Kahn answered with a loud, "Come."

The door opened, and one end of a chrome metal serving cart was pushed through the opening by a young, mini-skirted woman, who placed the cart close to where Boxer and the other men were seated, then with a nod of satisfaction, and a quick smile to Kahn, she hurriedly left the room.

"Gentlemen, help yourselves," Kahn said, gesturing to the cart on which were two carafes of coffee heated by cans of Sterno, and the usual assortment of Danish and cookies.

Boxer went for the coffee; he liked it black, without sugar, and he also helped himself to a cheese Danish, though it was his considered opinion that short of going to Paris for any kind of Danish, the only other place to get wonderfully tasting Danish of any kind was New York . . . and the moment he bit into the one he had, he knew that his *considered opinion* was probably a universal truth. . . .

"Well, gentlemen," Kahn began, after all of them were settled in their respective places again, "I asked you to join me this morning for several important reasons." As he spoke, he slowly stirred his coffee. "Huge changes are in the wind, as a result of *glasnost* . . . These changes will affect all of our lives, especially the lives of the men in our armed services . . ."

Kahn continued to *speechify*, as Boxer often called any long-winded introduction by a politician, or high government official, before the main subject was reached. But it gave him time to discreetly discard the Danish, and drink the coffee, which he found surprisingly good. It also gave him time to think his own thoughts. He had, only a few short months before, returned from a very difficult mission in the Arctic, off the coast of Siberia. He did not count it among his more successful missions, and the nuclear explosion that took place some forty hours after he left the area was far worse than the catastrophe that had occurred some years earlier at Chernoble. . . .

"I now come to one of the main thrusts of our new policy," Kahn said. "Submarines, like the *Manta* and her predecessors, will no longer be needed." His brown eyes went straight to Boxer.

"That's probably right, but I wouldn't be in a hurry to make that decision."

"It has already been made," Kahn said. "The *Manta* will be dismantled and sold for scrap."

"With all due respect," Boxer said, placing the empty coffee cup and saucer on the table, "it is a stupidly precipitous decision, and I would be willing to put that in writing and send it to the individual who made it."

Kahn flushed. "I was warned that you're outspoken, Admiral, and so you are. But I'd like you to know that I was the individual who made the decision."

"Then you should have consulted with me, or people like me, who are in a better position to evaluate certain situations than either you or anyone on your staff."

Yost frowned, and Pierce bit his lower lip.

"The decision has been made," Kahn said, his tone indicating that the matter was not up for discussion.

But Boxer, annoyed by the situation, responded with, "So much for intelligent decision making!"

Kahn turned a deeper shade of red, but ignored the jibe, and said, "Your new assignment, Admiral Boxer, will be more investigative orientated than command."

Boxer looked at Pierce.

"Your position in the navy, though you hold the rank of admiral, has been, ever since you became affiliated with the agency, somewhat in a gray area," Kahn said. "With very few exceptions, your missions were initiated by the agency; therefore, I see no reason why your next assignment should not come from us."

"*Us*, meaning you," Boxer replied hotly.

"Admiral, your lack of courtesy and respect does neither you, nor your branch of service, any good," Yost commented.

"General, Mr. Kahn has shown a good deal less respect for me, and for the navy, by making a decision which he was ill equipped to make," Boxer said.

Pierce leaned slightly forward. "You don't exist on our rolls," he said. "The truth is, Admiral, you don't have any legal existence."

Boxer stood up. "All right, what the hell are you trying to tell me?" He didn't bother to control, or even mask, his anger.

"You're a stateless individual," Kahn said, obviously relishing the situation, "and therefore could be deported."

"You're joking!"

Kahn shook his head.

Boxer glared at him for several moments, then in a tight voice he said, "You will be hearing from my attorney about this, and I will go public with it . . . I think you will find that you have made another stupid decision, Mr. Kahn."

"Just where the hell do you think you're going?" Pierce questioned.

"Out for a breath of fresh air, and a decent Danish, if that could be gotten here," Boxer said, before he opened the door.

"Leave this room and you're finished!" Kahn exploded.

"I'm finished if I sit and listen to your bullshit," Boxer replied, and leaving the room, he none too gently closed the door behind himself.

2

Boxer left Langley, went directly to Washington, where he rented a car, and then he drove down to Admiral Stark's beach house on the Virginia coast.

Stark, formerly the Chief of the Joint Chiefs of Staff and the CNO, now lived in quiet retirement, enjoying the pleasures of reading, boating, and painting, an avocation he had taken up after Boxer had bought him a set of oil paints and several brushes for his eightieth birthday.

Even as Boxer turned into the driveway, the door opened, and Stark stepped out onto the front deck.

"Heard the car," Stark called out. He was dressed in what he called his "painting uniform," a regulation coverall worn by submariners.

Boxer headed up the steps, and vigorously shook hands with his old friend, mentor, and in no small way, his adopted father.

"Good to see you, Jack," Stark said. "Real good."

Boxer nodded, and followed Stark inside, closing the door after him.

"I was just about to stop for lunch," Stark said. "My

neighbor down the road brought me enough crabmeat salad this morning to last me a week."

"Sounds good to me," Boxer answered, taking off his coat and jacket. "I'll go up to my room and get into something more comfortable."

"Do that," Stark said, heading into the kitchen.

Boxer went up to the room he'd shared with— He bit his lower lip. It was too painful to even think her name. That was one of the reasons he hadn't visited here after his last mission. But if he had a home, this place would be it. Stark, who had no children, had already told him that he was his heir.

"I made a good fish chowder the other day," Stark called up. "I have some left over."

"Good . . . I'll have some," Boxer answered, and pushing the past out of his mind, he quickly got out of his uniform and put on a gray jogging suit; then he went downstairs and joined Stark in the kitchen.

The table was set for two.

"Weather is going to get mean," Stark commented over the soup. "Barometer has been dropping steadily since early morning."

Boxer nodded. He felt the oncoming change in the sinuses on either side of his nose, but the one on the right was more painful than the one on the left.

There was a long silence between them before Stark asked, "Are you planning to spend some time here?"

"A couple of days, at the very least . . . maybe more."

"Anything you want to talk about?" Stark asked.

"Nothing now."

"Ah, I knew I had something to tell you . . . Chuck called."

"From where?" Boxer asked. Chuck was his adopted

son. He was now the communications officer aboard the attack submarine, *Orca.*

"Subic Bay. Said he's been there for a few days."

Boxer accepted the information without comment, though it wasn't usual for a sub on patrol to make port.

"He said that he tried to call you in New York, and when he couldn't get you, he called me."

"Sometimes, I find it hard to remember he's grown up, and not the street kid that he was when I first met him."

Stark agreed, and pointing to the bowl of crabmeat salad, he said, "If I let her, that woman would move in here with me, and feed me to death."

That woman was Mrs. Martinez, a widow, some ten years younger than Stark, who wasn't the least bit shy about displaying her interest in Stark.

"Some people would consider that not a bad way to go," Boxer commented.

Stark pointed his finger at Boxer. "She has more than an appetite for food."

"Really," Boxer responded, forcing himself not to smile.

"Yes, *really.*"

"You know what they say about the Latin temperament," Boxer said, enjoying the turn of the conversation.

"Not for me!" Stark exclaimed, throwing up his hands, palms out. "She cooks like a dream, and for her age, she looks like a dream, but I'm too old to fend off a sexual shark . . . No thank you, I'll eat her food, but I'll keep her out of my bed . . . And what I'm saying isn't to be interpreted the wrong way. I can still love a woman, albeit less frequently than a man your age, but certainly with gentleness and consideration that comes with having lived as a long as I have."

"Before you cast that lovely old flower away, have you at least gotten close enough—"

"I know what you're going to say."

"So?"

"So, I have already told you as much as I am going to tell you on this subject."

Boxer licked his lips. "This crabmeat salad is first-rate, Admiral. I'd advise you to think twice—"

The phone rang.

"No one calls here at this time of the day," Stark said.

The phone rang again.

"Maybe it's your lady friend from down the road," Boxer teased.

Stark glared at him, and left the table to answer the phone. Then he called out, "It's for you."

"Christ, no one knows I'm here," Boxer swore. Within moments, he was alongside Stark.

"It's the CNO," Stark whispered, handing the phone to his guest.

Boxer identified himself.

"Kahn is ready to go to the mat with you on this one," Admiral Pierce said.

"That's his right," Boxer answered, noticing that Stark had discreetly returned to the kitchen, and out of hearing range.

"To the President—"

"He's a political appointee," Boxer said. "You tell me what he knows about—"

"He knows that the word is out to cut his budget, and the *Manta* and all the previous boats you commanded, were partially funded by the Company."

Boxer had known that from the earlier days, when he

and Company's director slugged it out, or danced warily around one another.

"General Yost was less than pleased with your response," the CNO said. "He too is operating under the new budget constraints, and feels that the *Manta* at this time is a needless expense."

Boxer snorted derisively, then he said, "I really think my time and usefulness in the navy has run out . . . Besides, the last mission took more out of me than I thought it had."

"Before you put anything in writing, why don't we have an official conversation."

"When?"

"You name the time, and the place."

Boxer looked at Stark. "I'll be down here for the rest of the week . . . Let's make it Friday evening, about nineteen hundred, at the Washington Hotel's roof garden."

"I'll see you there," Pierce said, and clicked off.

Boxer put the phone down and returned to the kitchen.

"Coffee, beer, or brandy?" Stark asked.

"Coffee," Boxer answered.

"Coffee," Stark repeated, beginning to prepare it.

Boxer walked over to the rear door, and looked out on the deck, and beyond, where the bench dunes were, and finally to the sun-splashed sea beyond. Though it looked picture perfect, there was enough of a wind to send the waves crashing on the beach. Without turning to look at Stark, Boxer said, "I think I'll buy a sloop, and sail around the world . . . That's something I've always wanted to do."

"Good, I'll go with you," Stark said. "That's

something I never wanted to do, but always thought I should."

Facing him, Boxer asked, "'Should' what?"

"Sail around the world . . . I like sailing my catboat around here. But never had any desire to become a blue-water sailor."

"That's what I always wanted to do."

"You said that."

Boxer dropped in the chair he'd previously used. "That should take a couple of years."

"Then you could climb Everest, or paddle up the Amazon . . . Either one is good for another year."

Boxer squinted at him.

"And what will you do after you do all the things you ever dreamed of doing?" Stark asked, putting a mug of steaming coffee on the table in front of Boxer.

"Maybe join all the other admirals and generals who have become presidents and board chairmen of very large corporations. I hear the pay is a lot better than we get in the service, and the perks certainly are."

"And you will have become another sellout," Stark said, pouring milk into his coffee.

"Maybe so, but I'll be a very wealthy sellout," Boxer replied.

"You're very wealthy now, and will be wealthier after I die."

Boxer drank his black coffee.

"How much are you worth?" Stark asked.

"Two and a half million."

"With my estate it will be closer to six and a half," Stark said. "With that kind of money you can just sit back and let the money work for you."

"Yeah, 'just sit back,'" Boxer echoed.

"But you can't just do that . . . You need the action, the danger, and the real sense of doing something."

Boxer swallowed the remaining coffee from the cup, and said, "After I help you clean up, I'm going to go down to the beach for a walk."

"If you don't go now," Stark told him, "you won't go at all . . . That storm will break very soon . . . The clouds are already coming in."

Boxer looked toward the window. The sun was gone, covered by a sheet of grayish white clouds.

"You go, and I'll do the cleanup . . . You'll help after dinner."

"I'll do it all," Boxer said, getting to his feet; then from the hallway, he called, "I'll see you later."

"Watch your ass out on the beach. Those waves can roll completely over it," Stark warned.

Smiling, Boxer stepped out onto the deck, and closed the door behind him.

By the time Boxer reached the beach, the sea was running. Feathery tails of spume boiled off the tops of the waves, and good-sized breakers crashed onto the light brown slope of sand.

In a very real way, this violent aspect of the sea was foreign to him. His world had existed in the safe confines of a steel hull far below any surface disturbance.

Boxer mused on that thought for a moment, then let it slip away, and began to walk, high up on the beach, yards away from where breakers dashed themselves to pieces.

Over the years he had considered leaving the navy on various occasions, and for several different reasons. But this time, it seemed to him, was different. He was tired. His wife had died. He felt rudderless, and because of the advent of *glasnost* the role of him and his men had come to an end. . . .

He paused and, looked seaward, wondered if his Russian counterpart, Borodine, felt the same way, though he was lucky enough to have a wife, and now a child. His relationship to Borodine had become the strangest anomaly in his life. Beginning as deadly enemies, they became the fiercest of friends, even, at one segment of their lives, to being in love with the same woman . . . Boxer shook his head . . . That seemed to have happened so very long ago . . .

He started to walk again . . . He had always wanted to sail around the world . . . spend some time on a barge cruising the rivers of England and France . . . "I'd like to spend some time with Borodine, and with other friends," he said aloud, then silently he told himself that he didn't have to live on the edge of the knife all of the time. "Christ," he whispered into the wind, "I've lived close to danger practically all of my life; maybe it's time for me to step back, and live a more normal life."

Suddenly, a cold, driving rain slashed down.

Boxer turned and started to run back along the beach to the house. The breakers were exploding higher up the beach now, sending water spilling under his feet.

Before he reached the halfway mark, he saw someone running toward him. He wiped the rain from his eyes, and realizing it was Stark, he ran faster.

"Jack," Stark shouted, "the CNO is on the phone." He'd stopped, and took long breaths between words.

Boxer could hear him.

"There's been an accident—"

Boxer stopped in front of him.

"The *Manta* is down," Stark managed to gasp out.

Boxer ran back to the house, and took hold of the

phone. "Boxer here," he said, breathing hard.

"The *Manta* was involved in a collision with the supply ship, *Dee*, eighty miles southwest of Subic Bay," the CNO explained. "She's down in deep water."

"How deep?"

"Eight hundred feet."

"Casualties?"

"Several . . . Chuck is among them."

Boxer sucked in his breath, and slowly exhaled, before he asked, "How long have they got?"

"Their air supply is functioning . . . That's the best I can tell you."

"It's something," Boxer responded.

"The supply ship went down, and settled close to them . . . Jack, it's carrying a cargo of various kinds of ordnance."

Stark entered the house and leaned wearily against the wall.

"Can you arrange for me to fly out there?" Boxer asked.

"Yes . . . A helo will pick you up as soon as the snow stops."

"Snow!" Boxer exclaimed, turning to look out of the window . . . the rain had turned to snow.

"We'll jet you cross-country in a fighter, then to the *America*, which is on its way to the crash sight."

Boxer thanked him, and added, "I owe you one, Admiral."

"I don't agree with you on some things, Jack. But when the chips are down, as they are now, we're navy, and that means we're family."

Boxer managed to swallow the lump in his throat, and answered, "Yes, sir, we're family."

"I'll keep you informed," the CNO said, and clicked off.

Boxer put the phone down, looked at Stark, who like himself was so wet that he was already standing in a small puddle of water.

"Let's get into dry clothes, and have that drink of brandy, Admiral," Boxer suggested.

"Bad?" Stark asked.

"Chuck is among the injured," Boxer said tightly.

Stark put his hand on Boxer's shoulder, but he didn't say anything.

3

Boxer sat behind the jet jockey, in the air radar officer's slot. Ten miles down the ocean was very blue, almost black, and there were white puffs of clouds scattered far below, he guessed, somewhere between the ten and twenty-five-thousand-foot level.

From the time the helo picked him up until now, less than eighteen hours had elapsed. It was almost like riding the pony express . . . but supersonic jets were the ponies, and the distance wasn't across a continent: it was half-way across the world. The leg from the naval air station at Anacosta to San Diego was accomplished with three mid-air refuelings; then a second plane and pilot flew him to Hawaii, where he changed planes and pilots again, and when he arrived at Subic Bay, a pilot and plane from the *America* was waiting for him.

From the moment they passed through the twenty-five-thousand-foot level, the pilot, a Jg with the unlikely name of Augustus Maylee III, kept up a stream of chatter with the AO aboard the *America* that included everything from baseball to the kind of women they preferred.

Maylee, Boxer realized, didn't seem to be aware that his passenger was an admiral, and if he was, didn't seem to care. Up where they were, he mattered a hell of lot more than the rank of his passenger.

Within minutes, Boxer heard the AO report that they were on the ship's radar, and then order them to top off their fuel tanks before coming in for a landing.

"Wilco," Maylee answered.

"We've got some weather developing down here," the AO said. "We're in a heavy rain squall now."

The pilot laughed, and answered, "That's just to let you guys see how good Augie is . . . I've got twenty I come in on the first try, and take the third wire . . . Are there any real gamblers down there."

"I'll take your bet, but let's raise it to fifty," the AO said.

"You're on!" Maylee exclaimed gleefully.

The AO said, "Heads up, hotshot." And he began to vector Maylee to the tanker, a Gruman Ka-6 aircraft.

In a matter of minutes, they were topped off, and as they began to make their descent, Maylee said to Boxer over the IC, "We're going to get tossed around a bit on the way in, but we'll be all right."

"I'm sure we will," Boxer answered.

"Have you ever made a carrier landing before, sir?" Maylee asked.

"A few times," Boxer answered. "But none recently."

Maylee didn't continue the conversation with him, but he was exchanging terse comments now with the AO.

Suddenly they seemed to be riding along the tops of cloud ridges.

Boxer looked at the instruments in front of him. Most

of them were concerned with fire control, but there was an altimeter, which was unwinding. The aircraft was now below the fifteen-thousand-foot level and in the wooly-like grayness of the clouds, where the flashing red and green navigation lights threw bursts of eerie color along the tips of the wings.

"Niner niner, you have a condition three landing," the AO said.

"Roger that," Augie answered.

The AO reported, "Visibility less than half a mile in rain . . . Wind forty knots."

Augie acknowledged the information.

The needle on the altimeter was unwinding past five hundred feet . . . At three hundred they were out of the clouds, with rain splattering the clear plastic windshield.

They were in the groove; the *America* was directly ahead of them, and lit up like the proverbial Christmas tree.

Boxer could feel the landing gear snap into place. He glanced to the side. Below, the ocean was black. A jagged streak of lightning slashed down in front of them. The next instant they were hurled up, then, with an explosion of thunder, hammered down.

Augie made a quick correction.

"Call the ball," the landing signal officer said.

"Roger, ball," Augie answered.

Boxer sucked in his breath; they were going in.

The next instant, they slammed down on the pitching deck, and came to an abrupt halt, as the plane's tail hook grabbed the wire.

"Number three, hotshot," the air boss said from the glass enclosure of *Pry Fly*, the primary flight control, located a hundred and forty feet above the brightly illuminated flight deck.

Augie didn't answer. He was too busy following the directions of the plane handler, whose illuminated wands created momentary arcs of light, as he moved them to signal where he wanted Augie to move the aircraft.

Boxer took his helmet off, and cleared the sweat from his brow . . . Making carrier landings, which even the pilots referred to as *controlled crashes*, wasn't something he'd want to do again soon. . . .

Finally, the F-14 Tomcat was parked, and its twin jet engines shut down.

"Sir, are you all right?" Augie asked, before he opened the canopy.

"Yes, I'm fine," Boxer answered, then he said, "That was fine flying, Lieutenant."

"All in a day's work, Admiral . . . All in a day's work," Augie laughed, and then he opened the canopy.

As soon as Boxer was inside the island, he was greeted by Rear Admiral Gerold Kass, commander of the carrier battle, and Captain Jack Muina, the ship's skipper. This was his first meeting with them. Kass, a tall man with a bald pate, was in sharp contrast to Muina, who was of middling height and stocky, with a full head of very black hair and a well-trimmed moustache.

Kass returned his salute, then shook hands vigorously, and with a voice that emanated from deep within his chest, he said, "Welcome aboard, Admiral . . . I'm sorry the circumstances aren't happier."

Boxer accepted the comment with a nod, and Muina, saluting him, apologized for not having a formal turnout to greet him.

"Not needed," Boxer answered.

"While you're aboard, my quarters are at your disposal," Muina said.

"We'll discuss that later," Boxer responded, then turning to Kass, he asked, "Has there been any more communication from the *Tarpon?*"

"Hourly reports . . . but the situation has not changed much," Kass said.

"Are you in communication with them now?" Boxer asked.

"Only through the main communication center in Michigan," Kass answered. "This weather system forced us to abandon the communications buoy."

"We should be able to pick it up again after this storm," Muina offered.

"How long does the Met. Officer say this weather will last?" Boxer questioned.

"Somewhere between three and six hours," Muina said.

"Why are we standing here?" Kass suddenly asked. "I imagine you're hungry and tired . . . The RO seat isn't the best place to sleep, even if you have nothing to do."

Boxer managed a smile. He suddenly realized that they were just inside the ship's island, and that several officers from Kass's staff, as well as Muina's XO, were crowded into a very small place. "I'm ready for some food," he said.

"Just follow me," Kass told him.

Boxer trailed Kass up several flights of very steep steps, then through a door to his quarters, where stewards had set out on a table plates of cold cuts, freshly baked rolls, salads of various kinds, and cups and saucers for coffee.

"Coffee first," Boxer said, finally removing his flight suit, and sitting down at the head of the table.

"Suit yourself," Kass answered, sitting on his right, and while Muina took the chair on the left, the other officers arranged themselves around the table, according to their rank.

Boxer drank his black coffee, and almost finished the first cup, before he helped himself to two slices of ham and put them on a roll. He was about to begin to eat when the phone rang.

One of Kass's aides answered it, and said, "Captain Muina, it's for you."

Muina excused himself from the table and took the call. After listening for several moments, he calmly said, "Sound GQ." Then before anyone could ask what was wrong, he explained, "We have an in-bound plane with a landing gear problem . . . please excuse me." And summoning his XO, he hurried out of the room.

The next instant the klaxon began to scream, and as soon as it stopped, the 1MC came on. "Now hear this . . . Now hear this . . . All hands, battle stations . . . All hands, battle stations."

The men at the table instantly departed, and Kass said that he was going to the bridge.

"I'll go with you," Boxer told him.

Kass hesitated for a moment.

"I'll be better off there than here," Boxer said.

"All right," Kass answered, and headed for the door.

The flag bridge was one flight up, and on the *America*, and other newer carriers, it was below the ship's navigation bridge.

"Put the pilot and the AO on the PA," Kass ordered, his voice lost in a booming roll of thunder.

"I can't crank it down," the pilot said, his tense voice filling the bridge. "I can't get a green light."

"Maintain your present altitude and heading," the AO responded.

Lightning flashed off the port side and was instantly followed by an explosion of thunder.

"Wilco," the pilot said.

"Muina has to make the call," Kass explained. "He doesn't want to lose the aircraft, and he certainly doesn't want to lose the pilot. If the pilot ejects, it will be very hard to find him in this weather; if he makes a crash landing on the deck . . . well, we could very well have a major accident."

Suddenly the AO said, "We're taking you aboard . . . Dump your fuel . . . Keep enough to get you down . . . You have a condition three approach."

"Wilco," the pilot answered.

Suddenly, a voice came over the 1MC, and said, "All deck hands, stand by to rig crash barricades . . . All deck hands, stand by to rig crash barricades."

The ship's high-intensity lights came on, spilling bright white light over the deck, and onto the surging sea. Dozens of men worked the nylon crash net across the width of the rolling deck.

"Raise crash barricade," the air boss ordered over the 1MC.

Kass picked up the mike that put him in direct communication with the tanker's pilot, and said, "This is Admiral Kass."

"Yes, sir," the pilot answered tightly.

"Everything is ready for you down here, son," he said reassuringly.

"Yes, sir," the man responded again.

"By the way, son, what is your name?"

"Lieutenant Jg Donald Sing, sir," the pilot said.

"Well, Don, as soon as you're down come up to my quarters," Kass told him.

"Aye, aye, sir," Sing replied.

"Over and out," Kass said, putting the mike down; then nodding, he commented, "A damn fine man, damn fine!"

Boxer nodded.

The conversation between the landing signal officer and Sing came over the 1MC.

"You're looking good," the LSO said. "Hold her steady."

"I have a green light," the pilot responded. "Landing gear locked in place . . . I have a green light."

"Can you come in low for a visual check?"

"Yes."

Within moments the aircraft roared over the stern, and passed the bridge.

"Looks good," the LSO said. "Go for it."

The order came from the air boss to secure the crash barricade. In minutes the deck crew rolled the net up, and prepared to take the tanker aboard.

Boxer saw the aircraft break out of the clouds a second time, about three miles astern of the ship.

Now the conversation between the LSO and Sing was minimal. The LSO called for a slight correction to the left; then said, "Call the ball."

"Roger, ball," Sing responded. "Roger, ball."

Moments later the tanker came down on the deck, rolled forward, and before the tail hook grabbed a wire, its nose wheel collapsed.

The aircraft skidded off to the starboard, sending a shower of sparks into the air. Its left wing scraped the deck, and crumpled, spreading fire across the deck.

Instantly the ship's fire alarm sounded; then the 1MC came on, "All hands, all hands, we have a deck crash."

Kass left the flag bridge at a run.

Boxer followed him down to the deck.

The plane had come to rest over the catwalk. Heavy black smoke poured out of it.

Boxer and Kass were closest to the aircraft. Neither one said a word, but both of them ran to it.

With Kass close behind, Boxer clambered onto the plane's left wing.

"The latch to the right," Kass shouted, above the clang of the fire truck.

Boxer pulled at the latch, and the canopy opened.

While Kass came up alongside him, and the two of them helped free the unconscious pilot from his shoulder harness, the fire fighters began foaming down the plane.

Despite the smoke, Boxer climbed up on the fuselage, behind the cockpit, and reaching down, he pulled Sing up until his legs were free of the cockpit.

Kass grabbed hold of the unconscious pilot, just as a team of doctors and medics arrived.

"We'll take it from here, Admiral," the ranking doctor said.

Boxer and Kass maneuvered Sing into the waiting hands of the medics, and as they leaped from the wing to the deck, *Tilly*, the wrecking crane, moved into position to lift the aircraft up, and drop it over the side.

Kass grinned at Boxer. "You didn't waste much time."

"Neither did you," Boxer answered.

"Yeah, but you were there first."

The two of them moved away from the foam-covered aircraft, and watched *Tilly* drop it into the water.

"Now comes the job of hosing down the deck to get rid of the foam," Kass said.

"Won't the rain do it?"

"It will take some, but the rest of it has to be dissolved by a special solution . . . The deck must be operational at all times."

The 1MC came on. "All hands now hear this . . . All hands now hear this . . . Secure from fire stations . . . Secure from fire stations."

As Boxer and Kass started to walk back to the island, the men they passed reached out to shake each of their hands.

"I guess you're something special on this ship," Kass commented, as they made their way back to his quarters.

"Seems to me that you might be too," Boxer said.

And as they entered Kass's mess, they were greeted by a burst of applause from his staff. Then his chief aide said, "Captain Wilkens phoned to say that Lieutenant Sing has regained consciousness, and is resting comfortably."

"Well, that is good news," Kass exclaimed, and pouring himself a cup of fresh, hot coffee, he lifted it toward Boxer, "I'm proud to have you aboard my flag ship, the *America*, and I'm proud to count you, from this time forward, as one of my friends."

Boxer, filling his cup with coffee, responded, "You

said what I would have, but I would have and do welcome you aboard any boat I command."

The men at the table responded with a chorus of cheers, and after Boxer drank some of his coffee, he said, "If you gentlemen will excuse me, I'd like to get some Zs."

Kass detailed an aide to escort Boxer to the captain's quarters, and said, "I'll wake you as soon as we're on station again."

Boxer nodded, said, "Thank you, Admiral," and then followed the young officer.

4

Kahn, the Company's director, was livid. "Boxer walked the fuck out of my office, and now he's on the *America*—"

"And now," Admiral Pierce said quietly, "you're in my office, and if you don't lower your voice, I'll have to ask you to leave."

Kahn glowered at him. "I'm certainly going to discuss this incident with the President," he said.

"That's certainly within your rights," Pierce said. "But before you do, I think you should know that Boxer's son is on the *Manta*, and he is among the casualties."

Kahn shifted slightly in his chair. He was seated directly in front of Pierce's desk. After a moment of silence, he said, "So are the sons of a lot of other men, and they're not anywhere near the *Manta*."

"You're absolutely right . . . This is favoritism, and Boxer is one of the few men who deserve it. Hell, Kahn, if I hadn't officialized his transportation to the *America*, he would have gotten aboard her anyway."

"Are you telling me—"

"Before you say something stupid, let me tell you what I'm telling you," Pierce said. "Boxer would have found a way to get there, and there would be no way to stop him. Believe me, for everyone concerned, mine was the best way to go."

Kahn nodded. "All right, I'll buy it . . . Now let's get on to this *Tarpon* thing . . . We certainly can rule out the Russians now, and that means we can rule out sabotage."

"I agree, and I think we can also eliminate the possibility of it coming from another source . . . I've had the crew's records checked. They're clean, absolutely clean. Not even a traffic violation."

Kahn lit a cigarette, and then moved the free-form white ceramic ashtray on the desk closer to him. "You think we're looking at the result of some kind of a foul-up?" he asked, letting a cloud of smoke free from his mouth.

"Possibly . . . There have been an inordinately large number of accidents at sea and in the air over the past months . . . Our accident rate has gone through the proverbial roof. There have been accidents aboard other boats, but fortunately none of the boats was submerged when it happened, and none of the boats was involved in a collision with another vessel."

"Interesting," Kahn responded with a nod. "I'm beginning to get an idea . . . Maybe we can, as the saying goes, 'Kill two birds with one stone.'"

"I'm not following," Pierce admitted.

"Since Boxer's son is a casualty, maybe the father—"

"He's really an adopted son."

Kahn shook his head. "Whatever the hell he is to him, doesn't matter. What matters is that he is something to him; enough of a something that might be useful to us, and at the same time neutralize him."

Pierce asked for a clearer explanation.

"We'll offer him the opportunity to investigate the problem aboard a submarine, and give us a report."

"Have you any idea how many submarines there are?"

"We'll do two in each type chosen randomly."

"That certainly would tighten things up, if he skippered—"

"That's just it, Admiral, he won't skipper the boat. He'll be a member of the crew, but not an officer."

"You're joking?"

"Try me."

"What if he doesn't buy it?"

"He'll buy it," Kahn said with a smile. "A man like Boxer couldn't refuse the opportunity to save at least part of the American navy."

"Maybe," Pierce answered. "Maybe you've got a handle on him."

Kahn crushed the cigarette in the ashtray. "I have more than a handle on him, Admiral . . . I have him, here, in the palm of my hand." And he opened his palm, then closed it into a tight fist. "And that's where I intend to keep the famous Admiral Jack Boxer."

5

Boxer slept fitfully, dreaming about Chuck and about Francine. Pulled from sleep by the nightmare vision of what Francine looked like the last time he saw her, he bolted up to discover he was wet with sweat.

Suddenly, the 1MC came on, and a voice announced the changing of the watch.

Fully awake now, Boxer became aware of the low, constant hum of the ship's engines, and of her movement. He leaned back against the headboard, and realized that he had not yet come to terms with Francine's death . . . Maybe, he never would. But now it seemed fate was going to ask him to shoulder yet another tragedy.

Boxer left the bed, switched on the light, and was about to turn on the TV, and lose himself in whatever the ship's TV station was transmitting, when the phone rang.

"Admiral Boxer here."

"Sir, this is Commander Bains, the WO . . . we're due on station in forty-five minutes."

"The weather?" Boxer questioned.

"Fine, sir."

"Thank you, Commander," Boxer said, and putting the phone down, he shaved, showered, dressed, and was on his way to the flag bridge in less than fifteen minutes.

The ship's running lights were on, and planes for the first launch were already on deck.

The WO saluted Boxer, and said, "We have a helo heading to the communicaton buoy with a team of SEALS." He glanced at the ship's clock. "We should be hearing from them any time now."

Boxer nodded and glanced at the sea. He guessed the waves were two to three feet high, then facing the WO, he asked, "Has there been any additional communication with the *Manta?*"

"None, sir."

Boxer accepted the information without comment, folded his hands behind his back, and stood looking out at the broad expanse of the sea and the sky. Far in front of him, a dark, star-filled sky seemed to rest on an even darker ocean. He pursed his lips . . . When he first met Chuck, the boy was nothing more than a street kid, living with his aunt and uncle on Staten Island. Now he was an officer, with a future, and—

One of the phones rang.

A yeoman answered it, listened, and then speaking to the WO, he said, "Sir, the helo is in position, and has visual contact with the commo buoy . . . The SEALS are preparing to go in."

"Have them report as soon as they establish communication," the WO said.

The yeoman repeated the order, and put the phone down.

"We'll be on station before the *Hudson* arrives," the

WO said, referring to the rescue ship. "But we have special gear on board to pump air into the *Manta*, if she should need it. And we can send our divers down as deep as a thousand feet to assess the damage from the outside."

This time Boxer nodded, and was about to resume looking at the sea and the sky, when the WO said, "Sir, I took the liberty of sending to the galley for coffee?"

Boxer smiled. "That's a great idea . . . I hope you asked for something to go along with it?"

"I did," the WO answered.

"I'm much better after my morning coffee," Boxer commented, and he sat down in the second chair; the first chair to his right belonged to Kass, the overall commander of the carrier battle group.

There was more activity on the *America*'s deck, as lines of men, extending the ship's entire width, started at the bow, and slowly moved aft, picking up anything from a bolt that had come off one of the aircraft to anything else that might possibly foul a jet engine, and cause an accident. This "deck sweep" he knew, was done several times a day, regardless of the weather.

Despite the fact that the first launch of the day was about to begin, Boxer became lost in thought again. But this time it was about himself . . . Once he was finished with the navy, he really might buy an ocean-going sailboat, and spend a year or two sailing—

"Sir," a voice said.

Boxer looked to his left, and saw a steward holding a small tray with a mug of steaming coffee, and a good-sized plain Danish.

"The tray attaches to the right side of your chair, sir," the steward said.

"All the comforts of home," Boxer responded.

The steward grinned, attached the gray, and stepping back, he saluted.

Boxer returned the salute, and as the steward left, the phone rang.

This time the WO answered. "Sir, the SEALS have made contact with the *Manta.*"

Boxer left the chair, and started toward the phone bank.

"I'll have the conversation patched into the PA," the WO said, and told another officer to contact the ship's communications center and have them make the patch, then he said to Boxer, "They've lost all but one air scrubber."

Boxer could feel himself tense.

Suddenly a voice came over the PA. "This is Captain Greg Foster . . . We're not sure of the stability of the nuclear reactor. We've been getting erratic readings. If we go to emergency power, we will lose all power after six hours. Do you copy?"

"Yes, I copy . . . You are in direct communication with the *America,*" the SEAL answered.

"I'll take it," Boxer said, stepping forward.

The WO handed the phone to him.

Boxer identified himself, then he asked, "How hot is the reactor?"

"We can't get an accurate reading . . . The readout keeps jumping."

"What about the temp in the high-pressure steam system?"

"More than it should be by ten degrees, but that's within the safety limits."

"Stand by," Boxer said.

"Standing by," the *Manta*'s skipper answered.

Boxer rubbed his hand across his chin . . . If the reactor went critical, and the built-in fail-safe system failed to operate, they could have reactor meltdown, and an underwater nuclear explosion that could badly damage, and possibly destroy, all of the nearby surface ships. That was too much of a risk—

The door to the bridge opened, and one of the men called out, "Admiral on bridge."

Boxer motioned to Kass, and after repeating his "standby" order to Foster, he explained the situation aboard the *Tarpon* to Kass.

"I just received a message from the skipper of the *Hudson,*" Kass said. "She's running into the same weather we had a few hours ago, and because of it, her ETA has been pushed back two, maybe three hours."

"That's the kind of news I didn't want to hear," Boxer said.

Kass shrugged, and said, "It's Foster's call."

"No," Boxer responded. "It's my call . . . I'm the ranking officer here." And lifting his hand off the phone's mouthpiece, he said, "Shut the reactor down . . . Do you read me?"

"Loud and clear," Foster answered.

"We will plug in the Emergency Air Supply System, as soon as we can," Boxer told him.

"We'll need it."

"Have you started to shut down the reactor system?" Boxer asked.

"Yes, sir."

"Are the readings normal?"

"Yes."

"Good," Boxer answered with obvious relief. "Very

good . . . I'm turning the communication back to the SEAL on station . . . We should be there—" He glanced at the ship's clock. "Within twenty-five minutes at the very most."

"Yes, sir."

"Over, and out," Boxer said, putting the phone down, and looking at Kass, he added, "Nothing like starting the day with a major problem."

"Hell, you solved it, didn't you?" Kass responded. "That's more than most people would do."

Boxer said, "I postponed it . . . There are a hundred and forty men down there, and if we can't plug EASS in, they'll die, slowly, painfully, and in terror."

Kass's brow knit, but he didn't say anything.

"No, I didn't solve anything . . . I'm no different from anyone else, when it comes to solving a problem: I try to live with it, and hope that it will go away."

The 1MC came on. "All hands, now hear this . . . All hands, now hear this . . . We will begin the first launch of the day in zero five minutes."

"We have a couple of dozen nuggets aboard, who need as much flight time as they can get," Kass explained, as they walked back to the command chairs.

Boxer nodded.

"By the way, I stopped by in sickbay a short while ago. Lieutenant Sing is doing fine. He said he hoped that you would come to see him."

"I planned to," Boxer said, settling into the command chair he'd previously occupied, picked up the cup of tepid coffee, and drank it.

During the next few minutes, a total of a dozen Tom Cats were launched, one every ninety seconds. They would remain in the air for a minimum of an hour before they would land. Their tactical manuevers were executed at altitudes above thirty-five thousand feet, and at distances of more than a hundred miles from the *America.* If Boxer had been inclined to listen to the chatter between the pilots, he could have either used the earphones on the arm of his chair to hear it, or have it come over the PA system. But his sole interest was whether the men on the *Manta* could be saved before some unforeseen event occurred, and killed all of them.

Boxer, despite his dark thoughts, could not help but be aware of the pink flush of dawn growing brighter and brighter on the horizon . . . He didn't believe in omens, but maybe . . . just maybe this time the birth of a beautiful morning held the promise of life . . . life for the men trapped eight hundred feet below the surface of a lovely blue sea. . . .

Captain Foster, a tall, lean black man, with Indian-like features that stemmed from his Chickasaw great-grandfather, carefully monitored the *Manta*'s main instrument panel. The reactor was in the process of being shut down . . . All of the readings were within an acceptable operational level. . . .

"Target . . . Bearing, two eight two . . . Range, ten miles," the sonar operator called out.

Foster's concentration was broken. He turned toward his XO, Commander Mark Rogg. "Tell sonar it's one of ours," he said irritably. "The operator should have known that, and if he didn't then the SO should have." Despite the fact that he was exhausted and had a skull-pounding headache, he had remained on the *Tarpon*'s bridge since the accident.

"Skipper, we have our boat tagged . . . This is a new target," Rogg said, gesturing toward the bridge's sonar display screen. "It—"

A warning alarm began to scream.

Foster whirled toward the instrument panel. Several red lights were flashing.

A phone rang.

Knowing it was from the nuclear officer, Foster answered it.

"We have a malfunction in the fuel rod control drive," the nuclear engineering officer reported.

"Stand by," Foster shouted, above the piercing sound of the alarm, then looking at Rogg, he yelled, "Cut that fucking thing off."

A moment later the alarm's shriek was silenced.

"All right," Foster said, speaking to the NEO, "tell me what the situation is."

"The primary and back control drive systems are out," Rogg answered. "We're attempting to crank the rods into place."

Foster's black eyes moved to the instrument panel. "We're still running in the pink zone," he said, rubbing the bridge of his nose in a vain effort to reduce the pain.

"Yes, sir . . . Everything took a severe jouncing when we were hit, and when we struck the bottom."

"Just try to get those control rods in," Foster said.

"Aye, aye, sir," the man answered.

Foster put the phone down, and turned to the XO. "Better notify topside that we're unable to shut down our reactor, because the main and backup control rod drive systems have malfunctioned."

"Yes, sir," Rogg answered, then he said, "We still have that target."

Foster turned his attention to the sonar display, studied it for a few moments, and then asked, "Can we ID it?"

"No, sir . . . We weren't able to get its sound signature."

Foster gave him a quizzical look . . . As soon as the sonar located a target, the boat's highly sensitive sound system began to record it, and subject the recording to a computerized ID process, which took only seconds to complete. . . .

"The target was stationary when sonar picked it up," the XO explained.

Foster shook his head. "That's strange, isn't it?"

"Yes, sir . . . That's what I thought too."

"If it moves, we'll notify the surface people . . . Let them deal with it . . . Right now, we have more than enough to worry about here."

"That's for damn sure, skipper," Rogg answered. "That's for damn sure."

Boxer accepted the report on the latest difficulty aboard the *Manta* from the WO without comment, and without visible display of emotion. But the knots in his stomach tightened. He knew, all too well, that once a boat becomes snagged in a *life and death situation, other things begin to go wrong, making it seem as if death holds all winning cards.* He'd been in several himself, and had come out alive . . . sometimes, just barely.

The 1MC came on, breaking into Boxer's thoughts . . . "All hands, now hear this . . . All hands, now hear this, we are coming up on Alpha station, and will begin phase one of our rescue mission . . . All EASS personnel report immediately to the hanger area."

"It will take EASS crew at least a half hour to rig out the equipment," Kass said, looking at Boxer from his command chair. "Why don't we take the time to have breakfast?"

Though Boxer had no appetite, he felt obligated to accept the invitation. Besides, just sitting and waiting was beginning to get to him.

Kass led the way, and by the time they reached his quarters, the steward had just finished setting the table.

"I asked Captain Muina to join us," Kass said. "He should be along any moment."

Boxer nodded . . . It was going to be very difficult for him to take part in any normal conversation. . . .

"I sent a report on what happened last night to the CNO and the Secretary of the Navy, Albert Flint," Kass said, then he added, "I recommended you for the Navy Cross."

"That's not going to sit well with certain people," Boxer replied, sitting down at the table in the chair nearest to him. "In most government circles, I'm not the most popular individual."

"Yes, I heard stories about that, before I ever really knew who you were."

"The navy, as large an organization as it is, is too small a place for a man to hide in."

"Especially a man who does the kind of things you do," Kass said, taking the chair opposite Boxer.

Boxer flushed, and pointing to the head of the table, he commented, "The captain might be confused."

Kass laughed. "Not Muina . . . He'll take his seat at the head of the table without the proverbial blink of an eyelash."

"Ten says he stops dead in his tracks," Boxer challenged.

"Ten—"

A knock on the cabin door stopped Kass; in a whisper he said, "You're on." A moment later, he called out, "Come."

Muina entered, closed the door behind himself, and approaching the table, he said, "Well, I see you gentlemen have finally decided to defer to wit, charm, and good looks, to say nothing about youth." And he sat down at the head of the table.

Boxer looked at Kass, who smiled, and made an open gesture with his hands.

"Am I missing something?" Muina asked.

"No," Boxer said, "I am." And he handed ten dollars to Kass.

Reaching for a slice of toast and several slices of bacon, Muina said, "Given the appalling circumstances in which we are asked to perform our duty to our country, I think men of your rank should certainly propose that we are supplied the necessary feminine companionship to keep our morale up."

Boxer noticed that as Muina spoke, he buttered his toast with long languid strokes, and succeeded in giving the action a certain erotic tone.

"What say you distinguished gentlemen?" Muina pressed, straight-faced, and before either Boxer or Kass could answer, he said, "Take this situation, as an example . . ."

Boxer waited for him to finish, but Muina, by this time, was slowly chewing on his toast and bacon.

"All right, take this situation," Kass said.

Muina shook his head. "It was not mine to take; it was

given to me."

"Feminine companionship would have very little effect on this ship's morale."

"It would have a tremendous effect on keeping my morale up," Muina stated with a grin. "Just imagine, having two soft breasts to lay one's head on, to fondle, and having that wonderful tunnel in which a man's low morale can be brought up with exquisite pleasure . . . Gentlemen, it certainly gives one pause to think, and should give you, in your status, a cause to champion."

Boxer wasn't sure whether to take Muina at his word, or to laugh, until Kass said, "The captain should avail himself of the many gyms on board, or take several cold showers a day. Perhaps both would be necessary to temper his needs."

"To temper my needs, sir, would be to tamper with them," Muina quickly responded.

Kass looked at Boxer. "What's your opinion of the captain's suggestion?"

Boxer would have preferred to be a listener, rather than a participant, in a conversation which under the circumstances he found somewhat peculiar, but at the same time, mildly amusing, because of the theatrical way Muina delivered his lines.

Aware that he was the focus of both their attention, Boxer finally said, "I'm not sure it would work . . . You might just have the feminine companionship that some other man wants."

"Ah, that's just it," Muina responded. "It would make fighting cocks of all of us."

Boxer just looked at him.

"Fighting cocks—get it?"

"I get it," Boxer laughed. "But it sure as hell took a

long time for you to get to it."

"Touché," Muina answered, and then with a roguish smile, he added, "But sir, with all due respect, like the good fisherman, I was playing my catch."

Kass laughed. "You can always count on the captain to lighten the moment."

"Or make light of it," Muina commented, quickly stepping in.

"But being serious about it," Kass said, "women have played a vital role in the navy, and the truth is that, except for some of the more physically demanding tasks, they can do just about everything else."

"That's certainly so," Boxer answered.

"Gentlemen," Muina said, "I hate to harp, or to play an old saw, but, as the song goes, 'There is nothing like a dame . . . nothing.'"

"I'd be the last to deny that," Boxer responded.

"That goes for me too," Kass added.

"Then I leave the rest up to you illustrious—champions," Muina said, raising his coffee up in toast, "to do battle with the powers that be and bring dames aboard this ship."

Boxer smiled, and Kass responded with, "You'd be hard put—"

"Ah, but not for long, sir," Muina said, "not for long."

Boxer finished his second cup of coffee, but had little stomach for anything else, though he did pretend to eat by nibbling on a slice of toast. Ordinarily, he would have taken a more active role in the conversation, but the circumstances, and his recent loss of Francine, prevented him from becoming involved. But even if the situation were different, he probably would not have said much more than he had, though he had been sexually involved with many different women. . . .

Kass looked at his watch, and said, "We should be on our way, gentlemen."

Boxer anxious to get to the hanger bay, was on his feet before either Kass or Muina.

"Yes, 'there is nothing like a dame,'" Muina said, giving a parting shot, as the three of them left the table. "'Nothing looks like a dame, nothing thinks like a dame, and nothing acts like a dame.'"

"Thankfully, you didn't deliver that in song," Kass commented.

"Only out of respect for our guest," Muina answered.

"Captain, I doubt if you *respect* very much," Boxer said, pausing momentarily.

"Moi . . . Me?" Muina responded, pretending to be hurt and looking innocent at the same time.

As Boxer picked up the pace again, he added with a wry smile, "But then again, neither do I, unless it's worthy of my respect."

"Then certainly you respect the opposite gender, and—shall we say—the coupling that nature provided between their gender and ours."

Boxer nodded vigorously. "With every fiber of my being."

"Spoken with passion," Muina said, and looking at Kass, he added, "There's hope yet for mankind, and with the three of us loose, there's certainly hope for womankind . . ."

6

When Boxer and the other two officers reached the hanger bay, they found Lieutenant Commander Matenko's SASS crew had just completed reading the equipment.

Matenko, who was in phone contact with the boat's skipper, reported that the control rods were still jammed, and then he said, "There's just a possibility that when clean, dry air is introduced, the rods will free up."

Boxer looked at him questioningly.

"The moisture might be causing the drive mechanism to bind, sir," Matenko explained.

"But it's completely airtight."

"Yes, sir, under ordinary run conditions," Matenko responded. "But the unit's protective shell could have suffered a hairline crack, as a result of the collision, or even the hard touchdown on the bottom . . . A small crack, anywhere in the unit would admit moisture, and result in the condition that now exists."

Boxer nodded approvingly.

"Once we have a solid connection, I'll introduce a

small amount of very dry inert gas into the air line . . . Maybe that will do the trick."

"Good thinking," Boxer said.

"Thank you, sir," Matenko responded, and pointing to the SASS unit, he said, "It doesn't look like much, but it can do one hell of a job at depths up to three thousand feet."

To Boxer the underwater portion of the equipment looked very much like a stick figure. Its head consisted of a large steel ball into which was fitted several high-resolution video cameras with overlapping fields of vision, and zoom lenses, each with its own internal super-high-intensity lighting system that was computer adjusted for optimum visualization. Each image that was transmitted to the surface computer was digitally broken down, then reassembled to give the surface viewer not only an over-all view, but simultaneously, a view of any detail area within the picture.

In addition to the head, the SASS unit also had a long, pole-like body that ended in a trunk, which was equipped with treads that provided the means of locomotion on the sea bed. The device also had two arms, equipped with hand-like grasping devices. These were pantographically controlled by a surface operator. The SASS unit's right arm held a harpoon-like device, through which an air hose was threaded. Once the harpoon was exploded against a special port in the submarine—and there were several in the hull and in the sail—fresh air would be pumped from the surface into the boat.

"SASS will first make recon of the *Manta*, and the vessel that went down with it . . . Then a computer-produced visualization will come up on the video monitor that shows the three most accessible ports, leaving the final choice to me," Matenko explained.

The SASS unit was already in its cradle and swung out on a portable boom through the open hang door.

"It will take SASS four minutes to reach the *Manta,*" Matenko said. "But we'll be able to see the boat as soon as she comes within range of SASS's cameras."

Boxer accepted the information with a nod.

"Stand by to lower SASS," Matenko ordered.

"Standing by," the man answered from his position at the boom's control panel.

Matenko checked the various readouts on his console, then called out, "Lower away!"

The SASS unit splashed gently into the sea and quickly vanished from view.

"The boat should come on the master monitor in three minutes," Kass commented.

Boxer looked at the sixty-inch TV screen. It was completely filled with snow.

"Cameras on," a technician called out.

Suddenly, several good-sized barracuda swam across the screen, and then quickly vanished into the blackness beyond the reach of the light.

Boxer glanced back to where Matenko was. "Can SASS withstand a shark attack, and not suffer damage?"

"We can send a five-thousand-volt jolt down from the surface," the officer responded.

Boxer turned back to the TV monitor.

"Boat on camera," another man in the SASS team called out.

The *Manta* looked ghostly, and not more than a dozen yards from her the supply ship, *Dee,* lay on her side.

"Looking good," Matenko said.

Moment by moment, the picture of the *Manta* on the TV screen became clearer.

"There's where she was hit," Kass said, gesturing

toward the screen.

Boxer uttered a low gasp. At least ten feet of the *Manta*'s stern had been ripped open.

"Captain Foster reports that the boat's reactor has just begun to operate in the red zone," Matenko reported, obviously trying to control the tone of his voice.

"Sir, I request permission to abandon this mission immediately," Muina said, speaking for the first time, and directing his attention to Kass.

Kass looked questioningly at Boxer.

"I don't have the authority to make the call on this one," Boxer said, in a low, tight voice.

"If you did, how would you call it?"

"The way you must," Boxer answered. "The lives of the men in this battle group are your responsibility."

Kass put his hand on Boxer's shoulder, and squeezed, then he said to Muina, "Prepare to get under way immediately."

"Yes, sir," Muina responded.

For several moments, Boxer continued to look at the crippled boat, then he silently turned away, and left the hanger bay . . . It didn't really matter now, whether Chuck was alive or dead. In a few hours, at the very most, he and everyone else on the *Manta* would be dead . . . By the time he reached the flight deck, the huge carrier was under way, moving at flank speed.

Boxer walked to the ship's stern, where he looked out at its wake, which, like a white ribbon, stretched out far behind it, but never far enough to mark the *Manta*'s grave . . . That, he knew, would be marked for as long as he lived, by the picture of her he had seen on the TV monitor. . . .

7

Less than an hour after Kass gave the order to abandon the rescue effort, a towering mushroom shaped cloud erupted out of the sea to the west of where the *America* and her escort ships were. The cloud quickly climbed to a height of forty-five thousand feet.

Boxer silently watched the cloud from the flag bridge, and after it began to dissipate, he said to Kass, "I want to return to the States as soon as possible."

"Say when," Kass responded.

"Now."

Kass nodded sympathetically. "I understand," he said. "I'll have the same pilot that brought you on board take you back to Subic Bay."

"I have one request," Boxer said.

"I'm listening."

"I want to fly over the *Tarpon,*" Boxer said.

"I'll tell the pilot."

Boxer saluted Kass, and said, "You did what had to be done."

"Thank you . . . That means a lot to me, coming from

you," Kass responded, returning the salute.

"I'll be ready in fifteen minutes," Boxer told him.

"The aircraft will be ready," Kass answered.

Boxer hurriedly gathered his gear together, and went down to the ready room, where Lieutenant Jg Maylee, the pilot who had flown him out from Subic Bay, was already waiting.

The two exchanged salutes, and as Boxer suited up, Maylee said, "Sir, we'll be flying the same aircraft that we flew before."

"I'm not sure that I would have known the difference, if it was some other plane," Boxer said, pushing his arms into the long sleeves of the pressure suit.

"Sir—" Maylee bit his lip, looked down at the deck for a moment, then straight at Boxer. "Sir, I'm sorry about your son . . . I know—"

"Thank you, Maylee," Boxer said in a tight voice. "Thank you for your kindness."

"We'll fly over the spot at angle sixty."

"That will be fine," Boxer responded, closing the front zipper on his pressure suit.

"Ready?"

"As I'll ever be," Boxer said.

They left the Ready Room, and climbed the flight of steps leading to the door that opened onto the flight deck, where to Boxer's complete surprise a portion of the ship's company, Kass, his staff, Muina and several members of his staff, and the ship's detachment of Marines in dress uniform stood directly in front of the plane.

Boxer looked questioningly at Maylee.

"I didn't know anything about this," the pilot said.

Kass gave the signal and the formation came to

attention; then he stepped forward, saluted Boxer, and said, "This, sir, is our way of offering condolence to you, and showing respect to the memory of the hundred and forty men, who have gone to their eternal sleep beneath the sea."

Boxer nodded, and felt the tears rise in his eyes.

The ship's chaplain stepped forward, and recited the navy prayer for the dead; then the Marine detachment fired six volleys in honor of the men on the *Manta.* And finally, Captain Muina stepped away from his men, and taking a folded flag from one of the officers, he approached Boxer.

"Sir, this is the ship's flag . . . We thought you'd like to have it," Muina said, his voice breaking at the end.

"Very much," Boxer answered, as he took the flag from him. Then he said, "On behalf of the *Tarpon*'s crew, all of their loved ones, and myself, I thank the men of this ship." Then suddenly, the tears came, and shaking his head, he added, "Thank you again."

The formation was called to attention, and they saluted Boxer.

He returned the courtesy.

Then the formation was dismissed.

Within minutes, Boxer was securely strapped into the rear seat, and Maylee was maneuvering the aircraft to the number one catapult on the starboard side of the flight deck.

The aircraft was attached to the steam catapult's restraining cable.

Maylee went to full throttle, exchanged salutes with the Cat. officer.

The Cat. officer dropped into a kneeling position and extended his right arm toward the ship's bow.

An instant later the aircraft was hurled forward, going from zero to one hundred and sixty-five miles an hour in three seconds.

The Gs pushed Boxer back into his seat, and momentarily distorted his face.

Immediately, Maylee pulled the nose up, and the aircraft began its climb up to sixty thousand feet.

After a few moments, Maylee asked, "Are you all right, sir?"

"I'm fine," Boxer answered.

"That your first time off a Cat.?"

"Yes," Boxer answered, adding, "Submariners don't have much opportunity to go flying around."

"Guess not," Maylee said.

Boxer found the altimeter among the various dials in front of him on the instrument panel. In minutes, they were approaching sixty thousand feet.

"It's a short ride from here to that cloud," Maylee said, over the intercom, and almost before he had finished speaking, they were high over its mushroom-like top. "I'll circle it a few times."

"Thank you," Boxer responded, having to clear his throat before he spoke . . . With the exception of Stark, and in a strange, but very real way, his Russian counterpart, Admiral Igor Borodine, he now hadn't any emotional ties. . . .

"Sir, if you don't mind, I'd like to pay my respects to the men on the *Manta*," Maylee said.

"I wouldn't mind."

"Hold on, sir," Maylee told him. "I'm going to kick in the after-burner, and go into a three-sixty roll . . . Now!"

Boxer felt the sudden burst of speed, and the next instant, he was looking up at the sky. His stomach seemed to follow the rest of his body. Only after the third role was completed and the aircraft was level again, did he feel whole, and that took several minutes to achieve.

As soon as they left the vicinity of the mushroom cloud, they dropped to a lower altitude, completed a mid-air refueling, and then headed for Subic Bay.

8

Stark met Boxer at Washington's National Airport. "Thought you'd come home the same way you went," he said in his gravelly voice.

"No need to," Boxer answered, as they left the terminal for the parking lot. "No need to hurry about anything."

Stark didn't answer.

"I'll drive," Boxer said, slipping behind the wheel of the rented Ford.

"You look like you couldn't drive a kitty car," Stark said. "I'll drive."

Boxer didn't argue.

Neither of them spoke again until they were out of the city, then Stark said, "Borodine called to express his and Galena's condolences, and everyone from the President down has sent telegrams."

"I hope you started to respond to them," Boxer said.

"I had some printed letters made up."

"My crew—"

"To a man," Stark said. "I put their letters aside. I

figured that you'd want to answer them personally."

"Yes, I want to do that," Boxer said, then reaching over to the radio, he switched it on, found a station playing Mozart's Jupiter Symphony, and closing his eyes, he rested.

"Chuck's aunt phoned," Stark said.

"No doubt about the insurance money," Boxer answered, without opening his eyes.

"She didn't come right out and ask about it, but it was there all right . . . She wanted to know if Chuck had left any sort of a will . . . Do you know if he even had a will?"

Boxer opened his eyes, but didn't look at Stark; instead he looked out of the window, at the farm land they were passing. "I don't know what he left . . . We didn't have much of an opportunity to be together this past year."

"Feeling guilty about it, Jack, won't change anything," Stark said.

Boxer shrugged. "I don't know if I feel guilty, or if I just feel sorry for myself."

"A little self-pity is good for the soul," Stark said. "It's a lot like having chicken soup when you have a cold . . . It can't hurt you, and it might even do some good . . . It's only when you make the mistake of believing that a lot of chicken soup will cure you."

"I didn't know you knew so much about chicken soup," Boxer responded, almost smiling.

Stark scowled. "I know a great many things that you might not think I know."

"You just proved that," Boxer answered, closing his eyes, and resting again.

"I've been thinking about that idea of yours," Stark said, after a few minutes of silence.

Boxer heard him but didn't respond. He was still trying

to rid himself of that strange feeling that comes from spending long periods of time in the air—a kind of grubbiness, without being grubby.

"Sailing around for awhile might be fun," Stark commented. "Just the other day I saw an advertisement for a seventy-five-foot yawl."

"How much?" Boxer asked.

"Reasonably priced."

Boxer opened his eyes. "Stark, since when did you beat around the bush?"

"The man on the phone said eight hundred thousand—but probably with some bargaining we can get it for seven-fifty."

Boxer leaned his head back on the seat's headrest, but this time he kept his eyes open.

"Maybe, if you called Sanchez—hell, he might even know the guy. Sanchez is like that. You never know who he knows."

"That's true enough," Boxer said, sighing. "That man—" Sanchez had been involved with the men who had kidnapped Francine, but he, himself, had nothing to do with it. . . .

"After a few days of rest—"

"I'm going to take a vacation for awhile," Boxer said, "and don't ask me where, because I haven't the slightest idea."

"Good idea!" Stark responded.

"Yeah, a good idea," Boxer echoed, closing his eyes again and finally dozing off . . . Though it seemed like moments, it was actually two and a half hours later, when Stark gently shook him to wakefulness, and he opened his eyes.

"We're home," Stark said.

Boxer stretched. Every joint in his body ached. He opened the door, and when he was out of the car, he stretched again, before he went around to the rear, where Stark was already waiting.

"I rented the car for two weeks," Stark said. "Thought you might want to run around while you're here."

Boxer lifted his carryall out of the trunk. "Thanks," he said, shouldering the bag.

The two of them marched up to the front door, and Stark, unlocking it, commented, "I thought we'd go to Phil's for dinner."

Boxer nodded . . . Phil's was a combination restaurant-bar. The locals went there for dinner, or to sit at the bar, drink and watch a ball game, a fight or just shmooze away the time.

"The food is good . . . Not great, but good," Stark continued.

"I'll buy that," Boxer said, dropping his bag to the floor. He looked at the pile of telegrams and letters on the small foyer table.

"There's more in the living room," Stark told him, adding, "I wouldn't have thought you knew so many people!"

"Neither would I—"

The ring of the phone stopped him.

"You want me to answer it?" Stark asked.

Boxer shook his head. "Can't dodge it all of the time," he said and lifted the phone.

The overseas operator spoke, saying Borodine was on the line.

"Igor, you're the one person I wanted to hear from," Boxer said, as soon as his friend came on the line.

"Are you all right?" Borodine asked, speaking English.

"Not too wonderful at this time," Boxer answered frankly.

"Maybe, when I see you—"

"You're coming here?" Boxer questioned.

"Yes . . . In two weeks, I will be in Washington . . . First, to serve as the chief advisor to the ambassador for the Underwater Weapons Limitations Treaty conferences, then as Chief Naval Attaché."

"That's wonderful, Igor . . . are Galena and the baby coming with you?"

"They'll follow in six weeks . . . Jack, I don't really know what to say to you."

"I understand."

"I arrive on the eighteenth," Borodine said. "You'll be able to reach me at the embassy or at the Watergate."

"Listen, I might not call you immediately. I'm going to take some time for myself. Maybe a couple of weeks or so on one of those Caribbean islands."

"A very good idea. A rest will do you a world of good. You call when you come back. Have a good rest, Jack. You've earned it. See you soon."

"See you," Boxer said, putting down the phone. For a moment he stood motionless and looked at it.

"Jack, anything wrong?" Stark asked.

Boxer looked at him. "You and Igor are my best friends, and when I think of the number of times I had tried to kill him, I get goose bumps all over me. Christ, that man is my other self. If I had been successful, if I had killed him, I'd have killed part of me."

"But you didn't," Stark answered in the soft but distinctly gravelly voice of his. "Not too many in our calling ever get to meet, let alone establish a deep and lasting friendship with our adversary."

Boxer accepted Stark's response without comment, and picking up his shoulder bag, he climbed the steps to his room. When he reached the top, he called down to Stark, "I need to shower, then sleep for a few hours before I do anything."

"I'm in no rush to do anything."

"Okay if we go to dinner around eight?" Boxer asked.

"Fine with me," Stark answered.

Boxer entered his room, dropped the shoulder bag on the floor, and headed for the shower. In a matter of minutes, he was luxuriating under a torrent of pulsating hot water that relaxed the tightness in his arms, legs, and back. But the water did nothing to wash away the despair that, like a bank of dark gray clouds hovering over a calm sea, held the threat of a severe storm.

After Boxer showered and toweled himself dry, he slipped on a blue terrycloth robe, pulled back the white bedspread, and, stretching out on the bed, dropped quickly into a deep sleep.

After Boxer went upstairs, Stark went into the kitchen and brewed a cup of strong tea for himself. Concerned about Boxer, he wasn't sure what to do to help the man, who over the years had become his son, as much as Chuck had been Boxer's, though he himself had never legally adopted Boxer, as Boxer had Chuck. He had watched Boxer develop over the years from the skipper of a nuclear attack submarine to an admiral, a specialist in undersea warfare and technology matched only by Borodine. But now, Boxer was as close to a breakdown as he had ever seen him. He had slammed the door on the navy, and circumstances had slammed the door on him.

The phone rang, and before it could ring a second time, Stark answered it.

Admiral Pierce, the CNO, quickly identified himself, and asked to speak with Boxer.

"He's asleep, now," Stark answered.

"How is he?" Pierce asked.

"Depressed."

"Do you think he could come up to Washington in a few days . . . In two weeks, say?"

"He's planning to go on a vacation."

"Where?"

"An island in the Caribbean," Stark answered.

"All right, but I want him back here in two weeks," Pierce said.

"Is that an order?"

"A request."

Stark smiled. "He might honor it, put that way."

"It's important," Pierce said. "He might be able to prevent another accident like the one that killed Chuck."

"You want to tell me more so I can tell him?"

"Can't. This is all on a need-to-know basis, and secondly, we're still gathering data."

"I'll talk to him," Stark answered.

"Tell him I called to extend my personal condolence," the CNO said.

"I'll tell him," Stark replied, and put the phone down . . . As far as he was concerned the best antidote for depression was work, and if Pierce had something that Jack could sink his teeth into, it could very well spell the difference between a vital, functioning human being and one who lives on the periphery of life. . . .

* * *

Phil's had a gray, weather-beaten exterior, and an old whaleboat mounted on one side, or at least half of an old whaleboat complete with two carved wooden figures: the rower and the harpooner, holding his deadly weapon in his right hand.

Boxer pulled into the parking lot and said, "Looks like he's crowded tonight." He was referring to the number of parked cars.

"No more than usual," Stark answered, as the two of them left the car. "This is a popular spot around here."

They entered the dimly lit taproom, where one wall was lined with huge fish tanks, in which a variety of brilliantly colored fresh- and saltwater fish swam. Two other walls were given over to the display of various pieces of nautical memorabilia. The fourth wall was mirrored, and was behind a very long mahogany bar, complete with a brass footrail. And nearby, on the sawdust-covered floor, brass spitoons were spaced at intervals along the bottom of the bar.

The restaurant was located in an adjacent room. It was large enough to serve a hundred and fifty people without giving any of the diners the feeling that it was crowded.

Boxer headed for two empty stools almost at the center of the bar. "A Stoli and—"

"I'll have a Stoli too," Stark said.

"On the rocks?" the barkeep asked.

"Straight up for me," Boxer answered.

"On the rocks with a twist of lime," Stark told the man.

Boxer looked around. There was the usual mix of people. Some of the women were attractive, but none really eye-catching. As for the men, they were business types, though some were older, more in Stark's age group than in his. And there were a few young ones, probably in their early twenties.

The barkeep set their drinks down in front of them, and Boxer put a hundred-dollar bill on the bar.

The barkeep raised his eyebrows.

"I don't have anything smaller," Boxer told him.

The man nodded and took the bill.

"What should we drink to?" Stark asked.

Boxer raised his glass. "To the men on the *Tarpon*, may they sleep peacefully," he said.

Stark nodded and drank. Then he said, "The CNO wants to see you after your vacation."

Boxer didn't answer.

"Says it's important," Stark continued.

"Probably is," Boxer responded, finished his drink and ordered another one.

"I'll call the travel agency in the morning," Stark said, and asked, "Is there any particular island—"

"Antigua," Boxer snapped.

"Antigua," Stark repeated.

Boxer found himself looking at his reflection in the mirror behind the bar. He had the odd feeling that he was looking at a stranger—a man whose eyes betrayed his weariness, a man who, though not stooped, seemed bent under the weight of some enormous burden, a man—

The sudden roar of several motorcycles outside vibrated through the room, as the bikers stopped and gunned the engines of their bikes to announce their arrival.

"Christ, I was hoping they wouldn't come back," the barkeep commented, as he handed Boxer his drink.

Boxer saw their reflection in the mirror. There were four of them, complete with black leather jackets and

German helmets decorated with Iron Crosses.

They came up to the bar, settled next to Boxer, and one of them, a short man with long blond hair, demanded immediate service.

The barkeep had just switched on the TV, and the evening news came on with the story of the *Tarpon.*

"Hey, man," another biker called out to the barkeep, "turn to another station . . . We don't want to hear about shitheads."

"What did you say?" Boxer asked.

Stark touched his arm. "Let it go, Jack," he said in a low voice.

"Shitheads," the biker repeated, pointing to the TV, where a navy file film of the *Tarpon* was being shown. "The guys on board that sub . . . Shitheads."

Boxer put down his drink, nodded, and said, "If you really want to see shitheads, I suggest you look at your own reflection, and those of your friends, in the mirror."

The biker gave him a quizzical look.

"You and your friends are the shitheads," Boxer said.

"Hey, guys, you hear what this dude called us?" the biker questioned. "Seems like, he don't have no respect."

"Seems like that, Lou," another biker said.

"Maybe we should teach him respect," one of the other bikers commented.

"Yeah, I guess we'll have to reach him how to eat shit, when one of us says, 'Eat shit.'" He looked at the barkeep. "You got any shit he could eat?"

Boxer smiled. "You have a big mouth," he said, then suddenly he grabbed hold of the biker, swung him around, and pulled the man's arm up his back. "Move, and I'll tear it out of its socket."

The biker remained motionless.

"Now, the three of you," Boxer said, looking at the other three, "take your ugly faces out of here before I lose my temper . . . Now!"

"What about Lou?" one of the bikers asked.

"What about this piece of garbage?" Boxer responded.

"You goin' to let him go?"

"Sure, when you tough guys are on your bikes, and far away from here," Boxer answered.

"We ain't goin' to forget this," Lou said. "We ain't—"

Boxer pulled Lou's arm up.

The man screamed in pain.

"I hope you don't forget it," Boxer told him, and to the other bikers, he said, "Go, now!"

"Do like he says," Lou squeaked. "Do like he says."

The three bikers hurried out of the room.

With Lou in front of him, Boxer went to the door. He waited until the last motorcycle left the parking lot before he released Lou, and without saying a word, he turned, walked back into the barroom, and sitting down, he finished his second Stoli.

9

Reclining on a chaise lounge, Boxer looked out on the cove where the mirror-like surface of the water was dominated by a huge black rock shaped something like a hawk's bill. The water's surface was disturbed by several swimmers, making their way to a raft that was anchored to the bottom halfway between the white sand beach and the hawk's bill. The swimmers, three couples, were also guests at the hotel. Yuppies, down from New York for a few days of sun and sea. He had met them the previous evening at a barbecue. Two of the three men were powers in publishing, the other a trader on the Commodity Exchange. None of them, he guessed, were much beyond thirty. And the women with them apparently held various kinds of managerial positions. All of them were attractive and had lovely, youthful bodies.

Boxer slowly slipped some concoction of guava juice, rum, and several different spices blended together with cracked ice. His eyes went beyond the cove, to its mouth, and beyond, to where the light from a blue sky, flecked with puffs of white clouds, rested on a turquoise sea. His thoughts were in sharp contrast to the ever changing play of sunlight and color taking place in front of him. There was a dull November gray inside his skull, a tangle of dark threads that had no beginning and no end. . . .

Then suddenly a whistle's shrill sound cut into his melancholy musings. Within an instant, he became aware of the lifeguard on the raft, who was frantically blowing the whistle and gesticulating wildly. Then he saw the head of someone between the raft and the rock, and beyond, a shark's dorsal fin.

Two men from the hotel were already launching a whaleboat. Boxer dropped his drink, ran to where they were, and helped them get the boat in the water.

"I'm going with you," he said, jumping into the boat.

One of the men was about to object, but Boxer gave him a withering look.

Within moments, the outboard motor was roaring, and the boat, bow high, raced toward the rock. "We don't get many sharks in here," one of the men shouted above the sound of the outboard.

Boxer didn't answer. He worked his way forward, taking with him a life preserver and a length of half-inch nylon line he found stowed on the bottom of the boat.

The head in the water became more defined. It was crowned by long blond hair.

Boxer looked toward the rock. The shark's dorsal fin was now cleaving the water between the rock and the woman in the water.

"Ease up," he yelled back to the man at the outboard. "Ease up!" And he made a slicing motion across his throat.

The roaring sound suddenly ceased, and the boat's bow came down in the water.

"He'll circle around a couple of times," Boxer said, pointing to the dorsal fin. "You ease the boat toward the woman, and get her aboard."

The two men looked at each other, then the more muscular of the two said, "We know what to do, mister."

Boxer faced them. "You fucking well will do what I tell you to," he said in a quiet voice, "or I'll feed the two of you to the shark . . . Ease the boat up to the woman."

"What the hell are you going to do?" the other man asked.

"Watch," he said, picking up a long knife that was used for flaying fish and turning toward the bow.

The woman was screaming now and thrashing wildly around. She had obviously seen the shark's dorsal fin.

"Grab the life perserver," Boxer shouted and tossed it to her.

It landed a couple of feet in front of her, and she swam to it.

"Put it over your head," Boxer told her, then turning to the men in the stern, he said, "Get her in the boat as quickly as you can . . . The shark is moving in." He handed them the end of the line. "Get her in!" And with the knife between his teeth, he took a deep breath and dove over the side. This was something he had to do. It was almost as if the shark and he had been fated to meet at this place, at this time.

He went down only a few feet, before he arched his body and headed for the surface. The water was so clear that he could see the woman's bikini-clad body alongside the boat, and then, as he surfaced, her legs were already out of the water, and within the next couple of moments, she was safely on board the whaler.

"Come back," the muscular man shouted. "Come back, you still have time."

Boxer didn't answer. The dorsal fin was less than ten yards away. He took another deep breath, executed a surface dive, and saw the gray, bullet shape streaking toward him. The shark's mouth was already open.

Boxer's dive took him below the oncoming shark. Then with a quick reversal, he was within striking distance of the fish's underbelly.

The shark suddenly turned up toward the surface.

Boxer drove the knife's blade into it, and with all the strength he could muster, he wrenched the blade down, opening the white belly, and bloodying the water.

The shark whirled around, but Boxer clung to him, feeling the fish's sandpaper-like skin bruise his arms, chest, and the insides of his thighs. The thrashing body crashed against him. He made another thrust with the knife, let go of it, and started for the surface. The pressure in his lungs made him feel as if his chest were about to explode. He shot upward. Moments passed, and the darkness began to gather inside his skull. He had been deeper than he had realized, and now the surface, with the sunlight pouring liquid gold through the water, seemed to move farther and farther away.

Suddenly, he broke water, and sucked huge drafts of air into his oxygen-starved lungs.

"Here!" someone shouted. A woman. "Here!"

Boxer turned, saw the whale boat, and swam toward it. The men were waiting on the side to reach down and pull him up over the gunnel. Behind them was the woman. He came alongside, put his hands on the red plastic edging, and pulled himself up.

The two men offered to help him aboard.

"I can manage," he said, easing himself over the side and into the boat. "Sorry, I left the knife inside the shark," he told them, and working his way to the bow, he sat down on the thwart closest to it. "Better get someone out here to pick up the carcass, or some of his kind might come looking for a meál."

"As soon as we get you back, we'll go out and get him," the muscular man said, and then he added, "I never saw anyone kill a shark that way."

"I never did either," the other man said.

Suddenly the woman was in front of him. "I want to thank you," she said. "I—"

"They're the ones you should thank," Boxer said. "They had you in the boat before—"

"My God, you're bleeding!" she exclaimed.

Boxer managed a smile, looked at the insides of his arms and part of his chest. "Just abrasions," he said. "A shark's skin is—"

"Aren't you going to do something?" she suddenly shouted. "Aren't you going to do something?"

"There's nothing that can be done 'til we're ashore," Boxer said. "And then all I'll need is some antiseptic and cotton. In a day or so it'll be healed."

"Hey, the beach is full of people!" one of the men said.

Boxer turned and looked. They were close enough for him to see Stark. And when they drew even closer, everyone began to clap and yell.

"That's for you," the woman said.

"It's for all of us," Boxer commented, then looking at her, as if seeing her for the first time, he saw a young woman in a candy-striped bikini that left little to his imagination about her body. "My name is Jack Boxer," he said, holding out his hand, and looking into her emerald-green eyes.

"Toni-Ann Bruatigan," she told him, with a toss of her head that made her long blond hair swirl from side to side.

The whaleboat ground ashore, and immediately everyone on the beach rushed toward it. The first one to reach it was the Wall Street broker. He reached into the whaleboat and plucked Toni-Ann out; then holding her close, he looked at Boxer and the other two. "Thank you—I'm sorry, I don't even know your name."

"Jack . . . Jack Boxer."

"Andrew Wall."

"Thank you again," Andrew said, shaking Boxer's hand vigorously, then he said, "Tonight, the drinks for everyone are on me."

Stark came up to the boat, and looked hard at Boxer. "Feeling better, now?" he asked.

Boxer smiled . . . The old man knew him better than he knew himself . . . "Much," he finally answered.

Boxer leaped down into the water and walked up toward the beach. Once again the people started to applaud and shout their congratulations. He was clearly the hero of the moment.

"Better get me to a doctor," Boxer whispered to Stark. "I'm bruised inside as well as out."

"You're lucky you aren't missing anything," Stark said.

"Lucky . . . That mother was at least a dozen feet," Boxer told him. Then suddenly he stumbled.

Stark caught hold of him. "You all right?"

Boxer nodded. "I guess I'm a bit too old to do that kind of thing."

"Well, now that's an interesting discovery, Admiral,"

Stark commented. "Considering you lived to make it, I would advise that you remember it."

"I'll try," Boxer answered, as he reached the door of their room. "Now get me to a doctor. I hurt bad." And as he entered the room, he collapsed.

Stark managed to lift him into bed, then he went to the phone.

10

Boxer suffered more from a combination of muscular contusions and the psychological aftereffect of Chuck's death than from any serious physical injuries. He slept for a couple of hours, and by dinner time was hungry enough to go to the dining room, where he was greeted by a standing ovation from the other guests.

The leader of the steel band, who also served as the emcee, said, "Tonight, courtesy of Admiral Boxer, there's broiled shark steak on the menu."

Again there was a burst of applause.

"How the hell did he know my rank?" Boxer whispered to Stark.

"I used it to get us reservations," Stark answered. "This is the height of the season."

Boxer smiled at the people around him, then helped himself to a generous amount of the double vodka that was in front of him. He had hoped for anonymity, but that was gone now.

"You should have told me not to use—" Stark began.

"It's okay," Boxer said. "I guess it would have been

something of a miracle, if—"

"Company!" Stark exclaimed.

Boxer nodded. He hadn't seen the man coming toward the table before, and guessed that he'd arrived sometime that day . . . probably on the afternoon flight out of Kennedy.

The man, a burly individual, wearing white slacks and a white sport shirt, with the front open to expose a hairy gray chest, extended his hand, and said, "Admiral, this is a great pleasure . . . My name is Clem Gifford."

Boxer stood up, shook Gifford's hand, and introduced Stark, using his former rank.

"I was wondering whether the two of you would care to join me and my companions," Gifford said, gesturing toward a table where two men were seated. "We're from New York—Staten Island, to be exact—and we're down here for a few days of sun and fun. And maybe to do a little business." And he winked broadly.

"We're down here for rest," Stark said.

Gifford smiled, and he looked at Boxer. "I heard you went shark fishing the hard way," he said.

"I wasn't exactly fishing," Boxer answered, trying to think of some way of politely ending the conversation. But then Gifford did it for him by saying, "I better get back to my friends, now, or they'll think I've deserted them . . . See ya around."

"Yes, see you around," Boxer said, and as soon as Gifford left, he dropped into the chair.

"That man is slime!" Stark exclaimed.

Boxer nodded, picked up his glass, and drank the remaining vodka.

"Will you have the shark steak?" said their waiter, Paul, a young black man who lived in the small village just outside of the hotel's grounds.

"Not me," Stark answered. "I'll have the seafood salad to start, a cup of fresh chowder, and the broiled grouper, with carrots and baked potato."

"And you, sir?" Paul asked, directing his question to Boxer.

Boxer was unaware that he'd been spoken to. His attention was focused at the table where Toni-Ann was seated. She was wearing an off-the-shoulder white cocktail dress, and her long blond hair was held back with a braided red band. At that instant Boxer felt that sudden ignition in his groin that he had not felt since—

"Jack, are you all right?" Stark said.

Boxer looked questioningly at him.

"Dinner," Stark said. "That's why we're seated at the table."

Boxer suddenly realized that Paul was hovering close by.

"Will you have shark steak, sir?" Paul asked.

Shaking his head, Boxer said, "Not on your life . . . I'll have one of those humongous salads."

"Soup?"

"No," Boxer answered, his eyes moving back to Toni-Ann.

"Thank you, gentlemen," Paul said, then added. "I didn't know you were an admiral."

Boxer smiled at him. "Listen, if you won't tell, neither will I."

Paul hesitated for an instant, then guffawed, focusing everyone's attention on them.

Almost at a run, the maitre d' came to the table. "Is anything wrong here?" he asked.

"I just told Paul a dirty joke," Boxer said. "I'll tell it

to you—"

"No thank you, sir," the man said, and gesturing to Paul, he hurried him away from the table.

When Boxer and Stark were finally alone, Boxer said, "I want you to look at Toni-Ann and tell me who she resembles?"

"Toni-Ann?"

"The woman who was almost shark bait," Boxer said. "She's at the table, across the room . . . The one near the window."

Stark looked at Toni-Ann, and asked, "Don't you know?"

"If I knew, would I ask you?"

"My former secretary, Cynthia Lowe," Stark answered.

Boxer felt the color come into his cheeks, and he said, "She was a good woman."

"You weren't exactly the best thing for her," Stark commented.

"No, I wasn't," Boxer agreed. "But she knew what she was getting . . . I let her know from the beginning what I wanted and what I could give."

"She was in love with you."

Boxer shrugged. "I liked her, and she was wonderful in bed—but, well, I don't have to tell you how strange love is, or to be more accurate, 'what fools we mortals be' when it comes to love." Boxer looked around for Paul, and said, "I need another vodka, or the next thing that will happen, I'll begin to philosophize on the stupid things we do and then try to justify them."

"Another vodka won't change things," Stark commented. "Whatever was stupid will remain stupid."

For several moments Boxer looked at his friend, then he said, "All right, no more vodka." And picking up a glass of water, he toasted, "To Cynthia Lowe, may she be happy wherever she is."

"I'll drink to that," Stark responded, as he lifted his glass of water.

"Do you know what the problem really is?" Boxer asked, setting the water glass down on the table, and before Stark could answer, Boxer started to say, "The women I have known were too—" But even as he was speaking, he looked at Toni-Ann, and saw that she and Andrew Wall were leaving the dinner table, and were moving out onto the small dance floor, immediately in front of the steel drum band that was hammering out a samba.

Aware of how possessively Wall held her, Boxer suddenly felt a surge of resentment toward the man.

"You were saying something about the women you have known," Stark said.

"It doesn't matter," Boxer almost growled, turning away from the dance floor.

"Well, here's our dinner . . . I hope it's better than your conversation . . . I absolutely hate it, when you start to say something, then stop."

"Sorry," Boxer said. "I guess some things are better left unsaid."

Paul served Stark first, then as he placed a large salad in front of Boxer, he said, "The maitre d' wants me to tell him the dirty joke you told me."

Boxer squinted up at him. "So?"

"I don't know any."

"Neither do I," Boxer said. "But if you don't tell, I won't."

Paul gave him that familiar quizzical look, then guffawed again, but this time the maitre d' didn't come running to the table; he just glowered at Paul from where he was standing.

Hours later, when most of the guests were asleep, Boxer was on the beach, standing at the water's edge. The sky was full of stars, and far off, near the horizon, heat lightning shimmered across the sky.

Unable to sleep, Boxer had left the room, and wandered through the hotel grounds until he found himself on the beach. The episode with the shark was still fresh in his mind. That he risked his life, as he had so many times in the past, now seemed less than an exciting thing to have done . . . certainly less than rational. It wasn't even—

The soft sound of footfalls in the sand behind him made Boxer turn. Just enough light came from the tiki torches for him to see that Toni-Ann was coming toward him.

"I couldn't sleep either," she said matter-of-factly, as she stopped in front of him. Then in a much lower voice she added, "I couldn't get what happened out there out of my mind. What about you?"

Boxer, aware that she wasn't wearing more than a pair of blue short shorts and a red short-sleeved blouse tied around her bare midriff, and opened to reveal her breasts, took several moments to savor what he saw. Then he said, "The same, but from a different viewpoint . . . That was not the first time I killed a shark that way."

"I never really did thank you for saving my life," she said.

"That's not why I killed the shark," he told her.

She raised her eyebrows questioningly.

"You were already safe, when I went into the water," he said honestly.

"Then why—"

"This may not make a whole lot of sense, but I'll tell it to you anyway."

"I'm listening," Toni-Ann said with a nod.

"The shark and I were fated to meet, if not here, then somewhere else."

Without cuing him that she was going to begin to walk, she did.

Boxer followed.

"When?" Toni-Ann asked.

"When what?"

"When would you have encountered the shark, if it hadn't been here?" she asked.

Boxer thought about it a moment, shrugged, and said, "The shark was only the form it took. Somewhere else, it would have been something else."

Toni-Ann didn't answer immediately, leaving Boxer to wonder why he told that.

"I'm not so sure I believe you," she said.

"And I'm not so sure I can, or really want to, explain why that was the way it is."

"Still 'is'?" she questioned.

"Was," Boxer corrected. "At least, I hope 'was.'"

She gave a slight chuckle. "A girl can't even harbor any illusions these days . . . I thought you risked your life for me."

"I risked my life for me," Boxer responded.

"Well, at least you're honest about it," she said. "But had you, I would have owed—"

"Nothing . . . I would have been—I was going to say

happy, but that would have been the wrong word."

"What would be the right word?"

"Duty, I suppose," Boxer said.

"'Duty'?"

"Something someone like me knows all about, knows better than his own name . . . But even without me there, you would have been safe."

They reached the far end of the beach, where it began to curve around to form one side of the cove, and as they turned around, Toni-Ann commented, "The brilliance of the stars in the night sky is almost unreal . . . Look at that one!"

Boxer knew exactly what she was looking at because it wasn't a celestial body at all. It was a small chopper with a high-intensity light that suddenly began to blink.

Moments later the muffled roar of a high-powered motorboat throbbed against the night's silence, and beyond the mouth of the cove a dark shape cleaved the water into a white wake.

The chopper swung lower, its bright light dimmed for several moments, before it came fully on, sweeping the black surface of the water until its white shaft held the speedboat.

"What the hell is going on?" Toni-Ann questioned.

"Something we shouldn't be seeing . . . That's for sure."

"Drugs?" she asked.

"Probably," Boxer answered. "That chopper is off a mother ship—a supply ship—not too far from here . . . Maybe, fifty miles out at sea, or less."

Suddenly two men ran out of the hotel and down to the beach, and one of them began to flash a high-intensity light.

"Christ!" Boxer exclaimed, "right now, we should be any other place but here!"

"But—"

"If they see us, we're dead."

"You're joking."

"I wish the hell I was . . . Get down in the sand."

"What?"

Boxer, already kneeling, pulled Toni-Ann down. "Make it look real," he said, taking her in his arms. "It's our only chance."

"This is crazy!" she protested.

Boxer eased her back on the sand.

"Let go of me," she hissed. "If you don't—"

He put his lips on hers.

She tried to twist her head away, but he was much stronger. Finally, she stopped moving.

"That's better," Boxer told her, aware of the soft, rapid push of her partially exposed bare breasts against his chest.

She didn't answer.

He said, "They're still there."

In a low, angry voice, she called him an animal.

This time it was Boxer who didn't answer.

"Are you going to get off of me—"

He put his hand over her mouth. "Listen," he said sharply. "This afternoon I had a chance against the shark, but I don't stand a snowball's chance in hell of staying alive if—" Suddenly he saw the beam of light swing toward them. "You better be a damn good actress, or we're both dead!" He lifted his hand from her mouth, used it to open her blouse, and began kissing her bare breasts.

The cone of white light fluttered over them, and as it

lingered a moment, Boxer purposefully raised his head. An instant later the light went out.

"Now will you let me up?" Toni-Ann asked.

"Not until they're off the beach," Boxer answered.

Several moments passed.

"Now?' she questioned.

He rolled off of her, and scrambling to his feet, he reached down to help her up.

"I can manage."

Despite her obvious anger, he took hold of her hand, and holding it tightly, he pulled her up.

"Now, if you don't mind," she said haughtily, "I'll go back to the hotel."

"We'll go back together," he snapped.

"Is that one of your orders, Admiral?"

"If it has to be, it will be."

As they cut a diagonal across the white sand beach to the hotel's entrance, neither one of them spoke. But just before they entered the lower rear lobby, Toni-Ann asked, "Did you see who they were?"

Boxer pretended not to hear her.

"At least tell me who the two men were," Toni-Ann said.

Boxer stopped. "What men?"

"The men on the beach."

Boxer shook his head.

"You're impossible, do you know that?" she exploded.

"That's me . . . impossible. I'm actually famous for being impossible."

She glared at him, gave a wordless exclamation of disgust, and flounced into the lobby.

Boxer watched her, and enjoyed looking at the gentle roll of her buttocks, as she hurried along the hallway to the stairway. He waited until she was out of sight before he turned around.

The mouth of the cove was empty, the roar of the speedboat was gone, and the chopper was nowhere to be seen. The sea and the sky were bathed in the peaceful beauty of the night.

Boxer took a deep breath, and slowly exhaled. Then, remebering how good Toni-Ann felt under him, despite her anger, he smiled, and speaking to the night, he said, "That's one woman you'll never know."

"Who told you that?" she whispered.

Boxer faced her. He had not heard her return.

"I don't like to leave something that I started undone," Toni-Ann said, looking up at him.

"Neither do I," Boxer answered, once again marveling at the unpredictability of women. "My room?"

She nodded.

He took hold of her hand and gently squeezed it.

Boxer had not been with a woman for several months. After the death of his wife, he lacked the desire. But Toni-Ann seemed to possess the magic to turn him on.

In a matter of minutes, they were inisde the hotel room. Boxer switched on one of the end table lamps. A cool breeze came through a half-opened sliding glass door that led out onto a sun deck. The room, the most expensive in the hotel, was decorated in bright Caribbean colors. A king-sized, circular bed in the center of the room was reflected in a blue glass ceiling mirror directly above it.

They faced one another.

Boxer drew Toni-Ann to him, and placing his arms

around her, he kissed her gently on the lips.

Her arms slid around his neck, and he could feel her body lean against his.

He kissed her more passionately, wanting to taste her tongue, and at the same time caressing the exciting convexity of her buttock.

She eased her lips away from his, and said, "I want everything to be in the open between us . . . No misunderstandings."

Boxer nodded. "Sure, I agree with that," he answered, trying to kiss her deliciously warm lips again.

"Listen to me, please!" Toni-Ann implored.

"I'm listening."

"I'm twenty-four . . . I have a three-year-old son . . . In a couple of months . . . Two and a half to be exact, I'm going to be Mrs. Andrew Wall—"

"The man—"

"He's my fiancé."

Boxer let go of her. "Why are you here?" he asked, more sharply than he'd intended . . . She was old enough, and certainly smart enough, to know what she was doing.

"He had too much to drink," she said.

"That doesn't exactly answer the question," Boxer responded, now putting more than an arm's length between them.

"I'm not married yet."

Boxer shook his head. "That's kind of thin . . . You're with the man. You share his bed."

Toni-Ann walked to the sliding door, opened it all the way, and looked out at the silent cove, now silvered by a moon that had risen just a few minutes before.

"Andrew is a dear man," she said. "He's wonderful

with Keith, my son, and he's very generous to me."

"Seems ideal," Boxer commented.

She turned and faced him. "He's deadly dull in bed, or out of it."

Boxer threw up his hands. "You has your choice, and you makes your pick," he answered, giving a bad imitation of a southern accent. Then, in his normal voice, he added, "We seldom, if ever, find everything we want in one package."

"I know that."

"If the things he can give are more important than—"

"Jack, I don't want to be scolded, or lectured to," Toni-Ann said. "I told you the way things are, because I didn't want anything to happen that would hurt either of us."

Boxer raised his eyebrows.

"I didn't want it to mean something more than—"

"A one-night stand?"

Toni-Ann nodded. "That's it . . . Just a one-night stand between two people, who just happened to be in the same place, at the same time, and want the same thing from each other . . . I can live with that, if you can?"

"Is that the way you intend to live—"

"That's a low blow," she told him, and added, "Maybe, this whole thing was a bad idea." She started toward the door.

Boxer blocked her way. "You used all my lines."

"What?"

"I'm the one who is supposed to be telling you that it's all just for now, for the time we spend together . . . Come the dawn, I'll be gone."

She smiled. "Oh, I didn't mean to infringe on your male prerogative."

"Don't worry, you haven't," Boxer said, taking hold of her arms, and drawing her to him. "I'm not that egotistical that I can claim proprietary rights to something that—" He suddenly didn't give a damn about explanations; he wanted her.

"Jack, I just wanted everything to be understood between us," Toni-Ann said in a low voice.

He nodded and kissed her passionately on her lips. They were very warm.

Opening her mouth, she gave him her tongue to caress with his. Then, breathless, she moved her face away from his and said, "I'm full of sand."

"So am I," Boxer answered.

Toni-Ann laughed. "Good, we'll shower, and we'll do each other's backs."

"I'm for doing a helluva lot more," Boxer said, taking her by the hand, and leading her into the shower.

Naked, they faced each other.

Toni-Ann's body was even more voluptuous than Boxer had imagined it. Her skin was very white; her breasts, almost hemispherical with a tracery of blue lines on their sides, a splattering of freckles on the top of them, and very pink nipples in their center.

Soaping her body, he gently caressed her breasts. His hands moved down her stomach and around to her back.

Toni-Ann offered him her lips.

He kissed her hungrily. The months without having the physical intimacy of a woman intensified the pleasure he experienced. His hands slid over her buttocks, then into the crack between them.

Kissing her greedily, he held her tightly to him, feeling the exquisite press of her wet, naked body against his. He opened her mouth with his tongue.

Using the tips of her fingers, Toni-Ann teased his scrotum.

"I don't think there's a grain of sand left on either of us," Boxer said.

"Not a grain," Toni-Ann agreed.

Boxer shut off the water.

"Dry me, and I'll dry you," she said, handing him a huge white bath towel.

Simultaneously, they worked on each other's body.

"Easy, you'll take off most of my skin," Toni-Ann said.

"Just doing a thorough job."

Suddenly, she stopped, took the towel from him, placing it around her naked shoulders, knelt down in front of him, and lifting his penis, she put it into her mouth.

Boxer was too surprised to move. Her lips formed a warm ring around it, while her tongue caressed it with light, feathery touches. He reached down, and pressing her head to him, he said, in a low, throaty voice, "That's wonderful, Toni-Ann . . . Just wonderful!"

She looked up at him, and slowly drew away.

Boxer helped her to stand. He couldn't remember the time when a woman did that so spontaneously as she had just done. "That was wonderful. Really—"

"There's no need for you to say anything, Jack," she said, putting her hand over his mouth. "No need."

Boxer nodded, scooped her up into his arms, and carried her into the bedroom.

"Put me down," she said softly, "and I'll fix the bed."

Boxer set her down, and helped to take the bedspread off, and then fold it.

"Have you anything to drink?" Toni-Ann asked.

Boxer pointed to a small refrigerator. "It's stocked with—"

"What's your pleasure, sir?"

"You."

"I know that . . . But to drink, I mean to drink."

"Vodka, on the rocks."

She repeated his request, and padded over to the refrigerator, while he settled down on the bed, and closed his eyes. Though he hadn't been near a woman for some time, Toni-Ann was just the kind of woman he needed, and suddenly he felt envious of Andrew Wall.

"Here, vodka on the rocks," Toni-Ann said.

Boxer opened his eyes.

She was setting a tray, complete with a bottle of vodka, two glasses and a small ice bucket, down on the table. Her naked body was reflected in the mirror above them, and in the one on the wall behind the dresser.

"Later," Boxer said. "Now I want you." He held out his arms toward her.

She came to him.

"Do you want me to close the light?" he asked.

She smiled at him. "There's nothing I'd do in the dark, that I wouldn't do with the light on . . . Besides, if you close it, how will we be able to see ourselves up there." And she pointed to the mirror above the bed.

He nodded, eased her head down on the pillow, and kissed her passionately, while his right hand caressed her breasts. He kissed the side of her neck, then her nipples.

"Feels good," she whispered.

"Tastes good too," he said, lifting his face for a moment before burying it in the hollow of her stomach.

Her fingers moved through his hair.

Boxer eased himself down, and splaying her naked

thighs, he looked at the wet lips of her sex. For some inexplicable reason, they were more beautiful to him than he would have imagined. He pressed his mouth against the opening between them and used his tongue.

Toni-Ann made a soft, purring sound.

Boxer eased himself over her, and instantly he felt the exquisite warmth of her lips circle his penis. Avidly, he devoured her, while she did the same to him.

"I want you inside of me," Toni-Ann moaned. "Oh God, I want you deep inside of me!"

Boxer rolled off of her and turned around.

11

Boxer slept late, and when he joined Stark on the beach, it was already the middle of the morning.

"Had breakfast?" Stark asked.

Boxer shook his head. "Coffee and doughnut . . . It's enough until lunch."

"Seems like we're the only ones down here," Stark commented.

"I can see that . . . Where is everyone?"

"On some sort of a cruise around the island . . . Mr. Wall arranged to hire a two-masted schooner for the day and invited anyone who wanted to go."

"You didn't?"

"I'm here, ain't I?"

Boxer ignored Stark's testiness. Ever since he could remember, the man was always that way in the morning. He definitely wasn't a morning person. Sometime around mid-day his fires began to burn.

"You going to stay, or do you have other plans?" Stark asked.

Boxer was about to settle in the chaise next to Stark,

when he saw Gifford and the two men with him. "Looks like we're not going to be alone."

Stark looked back toward the hotel, then at Boxer, and pulled a face.

"Hey, don't blame me . . . I didn't invite them . . . Pretend you're sleeping, reading—"

Gifford waved to them.

"The man looks like a frog dressed in red trunks," Stark commented.

"He does at that," Boxer agreed.

"Top of the mornin' to ya," Gifford said, smiling broadly.

Boxer responded with a courteous, "Good morning, gentlemen."

"Mind if me and my friends join you two gents?" Gifford asked.

Despite the look of disgust that flashed on Stark's face, Boxer made a broad gesture, and said, "Suit yourselves."

As soon as Gifford was settled, he offered cigars to everyone. "I have these made for me . . . Cuban tobacco . . . The best . . . I have them made in Canada."

"I get mine through my Russian friend," Boxer said. "It's courtesy that's allowed between our government and the Russian."

"That would have to be Admiral Borodine, right?" Gifford asked.

"Right," Boxer answered.

Gifford took some time to cut the end of his cigar and light it, before he said, "Somehow, me and my friends had trouble sleeping . . . Isn't that right, Leo?"

"Right."

"Tony?"

"Had real trouble sleeping," Tony answered.

Boxer nodded. "That sometimes happens when you change environments," he said, not sure whether Gifford saw him and Toni-Ann on the beach or in the hotel. . . Maybe, even going to his room or Toni-Ann leaving it? Whichever one it was, Boxer was sure Gifford would play it to his advantage, if he could.

"I slept like a log," Stark said.

"So did I," Boxer offered, surprised that his friend had entered the conversation.

Gifford blew an enormous cloud of smoke into the air above him, then he said, "A couple of other people were up . . . On the beach . . . At least they weren't suffering from insomnia."

Tony and Leo laughed.

"They weren't suffering from anything," Gifford leered, "and even if they were, they were too occupied with other things to know it."

"Well, that's the way it is sometimes," Boxer answered.

Gifford nodded, blew another cloud of smoke, and said, "I'd like to believe that." Then he stood up. "I think I'll take a stroll before lunch."

"Good idea," Boxer answered, then he added, "Mr. Gifford, I hope you sleep better tonight."

"I'm sure I will," Gifford answered, and motioned Tony and Leo to follow him.

"What the hell was that all about?" Stark asked, when Gifford and his friends were out of earshot.

"Why did you say you slept like a log?" Boxer asked.

"Answer my question first, then I'll answer yours," Stark said.

"Gifford was on the beach last night with his two goons."

"I figured you must have been there too," Stark answered.

"So you gave me the opening?"

Stark nodded. "You needed it, didn't you?"

"I needed it, but he wasn't buying it," Boxer said.

"Someone with you?"

"The less you know, the better off you'll be," Boxer responded.

Stark shrugged but didn't say anything.

Boxer lazed the remainder of the morning away, then, before lunch, he swam back and forth to the raft a dozen times, and as he came up the beach to collect Stark, the air filled with the roar of an airplane's engines. At first, he thought that he was experiencing the effect of having gotten water in his ears, then he was certain it was the local helicopter out of St. John. But then to his complete surprise, he saw the Catalina flying boat, complete with United States Navy markings, come over the mountains, circle the cove, and come in for a landing.

"That's out of World War Two, even before!" Stark said, joining him at the water's edge.

The PBY came in, made a two-bounce landing, taxied, and then turned toward the beach, almost where Boxer and Stark were standing.

The ship grounded against the beach moments later, its props stopped, and two sailors left the portside blister to make her fast to the shore. Even as they secured her, a group of other men came out of the open blister, one by one. Several wore officer's uniforms, and two were in civis. Boxer immediately recognized one of them.

"What the fuck is he doing here?" he growled at Stark.

"Maybe he came down for the sun, or shark fishing."

Boxer said nothing, and as he continued to look at the aircraft, he saw the CNO, Admiral Samuel Pierce, who was the last man to leave.

By this time, not only were half the employees of the hotel down at the beach, but Gifford and his friends had returned.

"One thing is for sure," Stark whispered gleefully, "they're not here to see me."

Instantly, Boxer came to attention and saluted Pierce.

Pierce returned the courtesy, then Kahn, the director of the CIA, stepped forward. "I don't have much time," he said.

"Your problem," Boxer snapped. "I'm here on a vacation."

"The world doesn't stop because of that," Kahn answered.

"Gentlemen," Pierce said, "please!" Then he asked, "Is there some place where we can speak with some measure of security?"

"Our suite," Stark offered.

"Let's go there, then," Pierce said.

Stark took the lead, Boxer tailed slightly behind him, and the rest of men followed him. When he passed Gifford, the man snapped a salute. Boxer just glared at him.

Within a matter of minutes, they reached Boxer's two-room suite. The two men with Kahn took positions outside the door, while everyone else filed inside and standing, arranged themselves around the room.

Now boiling, Boxer said, "Okay, what the hell is this all about . . . I wasn't supposed to be in Washington for at least another fourteen days."

"Another boat went down," Pierce said.

Boxer could feel the color drain from his face. "Which one?" he managed to ask, despite the sudden tightness in his throat.

"The *Sunfish,*" Pierce answered, "off the Azores. Twelve hours ago. There aren't any survivors."

"What the hell is going on?" Stark questioned.

"That's what we want Admiral Boxer to find out," Kahn said sarcastically. "That's if he can give up some of his vacation time."

"We think it's either due to sabotage—"

"I thought the damn cold war was over, and that we didn't have to go looking for Russkies under our beds anymore."

"Maybe, maybe not," Kahn said. "But it doesn't have to be them either . . . There are at least a dozen other—"

"Spare me the list," Boxer said. "I know who they are, as well as you do . . . Probably better . . . I probably encountered several of them, one way or another."

"It may also be the result of a certain kind of sloppiness that sometimes shows up, when men become too sure of themselves, or begin to think that a dangerous job, however routine, is routine enough not to have to think about it," Pierce offered. "That happened back in '89, and we lost a lot of good men . . . Then it involved surface ships and aircraft, and the entire fleet had to stand down for training exercises."

Boxer nodded. "I remember," he said.

"Now we think the same thing—"

"Who's the *we?*" Boxer asked.

Kahn's face reddened. He looked as if he were ready to throw up his hands.

Pierce said, "Some of our information seems to

indicate that sloppiness is taking root aboard our submarines."

"We have to be sure that it's that, and only that," Kahn chimed in, having gained control of his temper.

"And you want me to check it out for you," Boxer said, filling a pipe and then tamping down the tobacco in the bowl.

"Yes," Kahn answered. "We want you to go in as a rate, get to know the crew of one or two—maybe a half a dozen of our newest submarines."

Boxer turned toward Stark.

"We'll buy the sailboat as soon as you're finished with this assignment," Stark said.

Boxer lit the pipe, and blew a dense cloud of smoke up toward the ceiling. He thought of Chuck, and taking the pipe out of his mouth, he asked, "When do you want me to go aboard?"

"Day after tomorrow," Pierce said. "The *Andrew Jackson* . . . She's in Norfolk now, and will go out on a routine training mission off Cuba."

Boxer nodded.

Pierce turned to an aide, who handed him an enlisted man's file jacket. "Everything you'll need is in here," he told Boxer. "ID, orders, and even your bogus service record."

"Will the skipper know I'm aboard?" Boxer asked, taking the file jacket from the CNO.

Pierce shook his head. "It must be a total undercover operation."

"How long do I stay aboard?"

"Until you're satisfied that the boat is safe," Kahn answered.

"I'll be aboard on time," Boxer said.

Pierce smiled, and shook his hand, then Kahn said, "We'd prefer it if you returned with us now."

"What?" Boxer questioned.

"It's just a request," Kahn quickly said.

"Request denied," Boxer snapped.

"God, you are a pain in the ass!" Kahn responded.

"That is part of my charm," Boxer said.

"All right, enough of that," Pierce told them. "I would have thought that each of you would have learned to tolerate the other."

"Why don't you stay for dinner," Stark answered . . . "It's served at six."

"That will mean a night landing in Gitmo," Kahn said, using the slang name of the Guantanamo naval base in Cuba.

"We've been doing that for more years than I can remember," Stark commented. "It's just another airport."

"All right," Kahn said. "We'll stay for dinner."

"I'll make the necessary arrangements," Stark volunteered. "I'll meet you at the beach . . . You've got some time to take it easy."

"Good idea," Boxer said, already leading the way out of the suite. "We'll order a cool drink and relax."

Pierce caught up to him and asked if he was all right.

Boxer looked at him questioningly, then answered, "As all right as a man can be, considering the circumstances."

"You look as if you tangled with—"

"A shark."

"What?"

Boxer waved the question aside, and said, "Sooner or

later, doesn't every man encounter his own personal shark?"

"I'm not going to pursue that," Pierce said.

Boxer chuckled. "Best not to," he said.

The group filed out to the beach, and headed for a group of brightly colored web chairs on which they settled in a rough semi-circle, open toward the cove.

It was close to five when Stark noted the two masts of the schooner just before she rounded the cove. Within a matter of minutes she came into full view.

"Damn fine-looking ship!" Pierce exclaimed.

Boxer and everyone else agreed.

The schooner, whose name was the *Kate I*, came into the cove, while her crew quickly reefed her sails. She dropped anchor just beyond the swimming raft, and two boats were lowered to take her passengers to the beach.

Boxer watched the operation, and commented to Stark that it was "smartly executed."

Stark agreed.

The small boats ground up to the beach, and the day sailors leaped or stepped over the gunnels into a few inches of water, and then scrambled up the beach.

Most were sunburned, and all of the women's hair had a wind-blown look. But they were laughing, and obviously had had a good time.

The small boats already started back to the schooner.

Toni-Ann and Andrew were walking arm in arm up the beach. She was wearing a red bikini bra, with a multicolored sarong-like half skirt covering the bottom. Her eyes flicked in his direction. She said something to

Andrew, and he answered her, then they started toward him.

Andrew offered his hand to Boxer, who shook it and introduced him and Toni-Ann to everyone.

"Gentlemen," Andrew said, "please be my guests for dinner . . . I owe Admiral Boxer at least that."

"You owe me nothing," Boxer said, coloring.

Andrew circled Toni-Ann's bare shoulders with his arm. "Jack—I hope you don't mind me calling you by your given name?"

Boxer shook his head.

"Jack saved Toni-Ann's life yesterday," he said with boyish enthusiasm.

"Please," Boxer said. "Please, don't bore these men with the details."

But Kahn insisted on hearing, and Andrew was only too eager to tell him.

"The men had her in the boat before I was in the water," Boxer protested. "Besides, it was something anyone would have done—"

"Nonsense!" Andrew exclaimed, still holding Toni-Ann around her shoulders. "Nonsense . . . Please, gentlemen, be my dinner guests."

"I don't see how we could refuse," Stark said.

"Good," Andrew exclaimed. "See you at dinner, gentlemen."

Boxer watched him and Toni-Ann walk up the beach. Suddenly, he felt completely at odds with himself, and said, "I feel like a walk. Does anyone want to join me?" Though he'd asked for company, he really didn't want any.

The invitation was politely declined by everyone.

Boxer went up the beach, to where he and Toni-Ann

had been the previous night . . . The idea of Andrew making love to Toni-Ann bothered him, though he realized that it shouldn't. After all, he was years older than she, and a *one-night stand* seldom made for a lasting relationship. But he was certainly put out by it. . . .

He reached the line of shrubbery that marked off the end of the hotel's property. He stopped, turned around, and started back.

As far as Boxer was concerned, there wasn't anything he could do to change things. Though Toni-Ann liked Andrew, she didn't love him, and was marrying him for the security he would be able to give her and her son.

Boxer pursed his lips . . . More than one marriage had an economic bottom line, and very little love in it. Well, in another day, she would be out of his life forever, and he would be aboard the *Andrew Jackson*. . . .

By the time he was close to the hotel again, only Stark was on the beach.

"The others went up to the suite to freshen up a bit before dinner," Stark explained, then he asked, "Feeling better now that you've had your walk?"

"Much."

"That Andrew really doesn't mean any harm," Stark commented.

"Christ, the way he tells the damn story, you'd think he'd killed the shark."

Stark smiled, and said, "I'm sure he would have liked to." Then he added, "In time, he might even believe that he had."

Boxer nodded, then looking at Stark he caught that impish light in the man's blue eyes. In an instant the two of them guffawed. Then putting his arm around the shoulders of his old friend, Boxer said, "Let's go freshen up too."

"Good idea," Stark answered. "Damn good idea."

Dinner was served on the hotel's wide veranda, just back of the beach. Tiki torches were set up, and their flickering light made interesting patterns across everything and everyone. It was one of those occasions that Boxer was forced to endure. He did not enjoy the adulation showered on him by Andrew and his friends, and he did not enjoy the small talk that made up the conversation at the table. The only thing that gave him any pleasure was to look at Toni-Ann. She wore a lovely green coverall, which was open down to the third button. Her blond hair was tied back with a piece of green ribbon, and her face and bare arms were lightly tanned.

Now and then their eyes met, but she always looked away.

Boxer noticed Gifford and his friends. They sat in lonely isolation at one of the tables located closer to the hotel than to the beach. Then, suddenly, Boxer saw Kahn look at Gifford, and to his astonishment he saw Kahn give an almost imperceptible nod. Had he not been looking directly at Kahn at that precise moment, he would have missed it.

Boxer's eyes flicked to Gifford, but the man was interested in the huge lobster just set down in front of him, and his face was turned down . . . But Boxer had enough experience with the Company and with Kahn's predecessors to know that men like Kahn and Gifford were more in tune with each other than he was with either of them. They could play on either side, if it suited their purpose. . . .

Just before the main course was served, the steel band began to play rumba, and before Boxer realized what he was doing, he asked Toni-Ann to dance with him. As soon as they were out on the dance floor, and Boxer put his arms around her, he said, "I'm leaving tomorrow."

"I guessed that was going to happen, when I saw your guests," she said.

He held her closer.

"Don't," she said in a low voice. "It will only make it more difficult for both of us."

"I didn't think it was difficult for you," he said, executing a side step.

"I'm not made of stone."

"Neither am I," he answered, pulling her against him, and holding her there long enough to feel the crush of her braless breasts against his chest.

"That's not fair," Toni-Ann complained.

"No, it's not," Boxer agreed. "But I can't always be fair, or courageous. I want you, and I know you want me."

She gave him a wan smile. "I learned long ago, Jack, that more often than not, what I wanted and what I could get were separated by eons of light years."

The music came to an end just as Boxer executed a dip, and after bringing her up, he escorted her back to the table.

Kahn was anxious to leave, and directly after dinner, Boxer and Stark went down with the visitors to where the old Catalina was moored.

"See you in Washington," Pierce said.

"Yes, sir," Boxer answered, rendering a sharp salute.

Pierce returned the courtesy, smiled and climbed aboard the aircraft, entering it through the starboard blister, swung open and secured for the purpose.

Within minutes the flying boat was throbbing across the cove, creating a white furrow in the otherwise black surface. Then the craft rose out of the water, gained altitude, banked to the right, and headed up over the island, flying northeast.

By the time Boxer and Stark returned to the dinner table, everyone had gone.

"No sense sitting here anymore," Stark said.

"Walk?" Boxer asked.

"Only if you promise not to talk," Stark replied.

"I promise," Boxer said. He'd intended to tell Stark about the silent exchange that had taken place between Kahn and Gifford, but decided against it. It wasn't worth the possibility of spoiling their walk. . . .

The two of them started toward the beach, and slowly began to walk along the line formed between the dark water of the cove and the white sand of the beach.

12

Boxer and Stark left the Hawksbill Hotel just after breakfast. He had one of the local cabbies drive them out to the airport, and they boarded a flight that took them straight to Kennedy, where they hired an air cab service to fly them into Washington's National Airport. There they separated: Boxer went directly to his hotel, while Stark drove back to his home on the Virginia coast.

The desk clerk handed Boxer several large cartons, which he guessed were the necessary uniforms for the character role he was about to assume. By the time he unpacked the clothes he had with him at the Hawksbill, and packed his sea bag with clothing he would take aboard the *Andrew Jackson*, it was well past six o'clock in the evening, and having skipped lunch, he was beginning to feel hungry.

Boxer had no particular yen for a special food when he left the hotel, and decided to walk until he found a place that caught his fancy. He wanted either a quiet restaurant or something like a mom and pop eatery.

He made stops at various restaurants to either look at a

menu or to make a quick examination of the interior. Neither the bill of fare nor the decor of those places where he stopped pleased him, and, hailing a cab, he told the driver to take him down to the waterfront, where there were at least half a dozen good seafood restaurants.

He chose the Barge, a restaurant that was actually built on a reconditioned barge. He was escorted to a window table that gave him a view of the Potomac and a small marina nearby. From where he sat, he also had a view of the oakwood bar, at the far side of the restaurant, and all the tables between, or their reflection in the huge mirror behind the bar. The room was decorated in a nautical motif that included several old posters that advertised ocean crossing on the *Queen Mary*, the *Normandie*, and the *Isle de France*. There were even several very expensive sailing ship models on shelves around the room.

Boxer lit his pipe, ordered a Stoli on the rocks, and contented himself with looking at the river traffic before dinner. The window framed half a dozen boats of various sizes, ranging from a small runabout with an outboard engine to a good-sized yacht that probably had a master bedroom, complete gallery and bathroom. Whoever owned it was stupidly creating a wake that bounced the small craft around.

The waitress, a young woman with thinly penciled eyebrows, brought his Stoli, and asked him if he was ready to order.

"Not just yet," he answered, managing a smile. "I'll call you when I'm ready."

She didn't look particularly pleased.

Boxer turned toward the window, and continued to watch the big yacht bully the smaller boats. It was also obvious to him that the weather was beginning to turn. The wind had freshened and had shifted from the west to the southwest. There were some thunderheads rapidly approaching from the southwest.

The longer Boxer watched the yacht play games, the more out of sorts he became . . . The man at the wheel was an idiot . . .

He drained his glass, then summoned the waitress.

"Are you ready to order, now?" she asked.

"Just another Stoli, please," he answered. This time he didn't smile, and as soon as he told her what he wanted, he turned his attention back to what was happening on the river.

Boxer soon looked toward the bar. He could define some of his feelings . . . Certainly part of it had to do with what he was now witnessing. But much of it had to do with Chuck's death, the death of his wife . . . the pleasure he'd experienced with Toni-Ann, and the knowledge that it was so short-lived . . . and even more irksome was the connection he'd discovered between Gifford and Kahn . . . For some reason, his thoughts seemed to hang there, snared by his dislike for Kahn and for Gifford. . . .

He drained the last of the second Stoli, and was about to open the large menu, when suddenly a woman at another table shrilled, "It's coming straight for us!"

Boxer turned toward the window.

The yacht—the *She Devil*— was heading toward the Barge with her throttle wide open.

Boxer's eyes looked down the side of the barge. There wasn't even a small landing stage between the barge and any craft that would come alongside. "Everyone," he shouted, "get out . . . get out!"

The people bolted from their tables and headed for the exits amidship and at one end.

Boxer moved back to the bar, hoping that at the last minute the crazy son-of-bitch at the wheel would swerve . . . Suddenly he remembered the crash between *Shark* and Sanchez's yacht, the *Mary-Ann* . . . It was all there in vivid color, playing like some video cassette in the VCR of his brain. The night was foggy. The *Shark* was returning from a long patrol, and then out of nowhere the *Mary-Ann* slammed into them. . . .

The *She Devil* crashed into the barge, shattering the huge window, and rocking her so violently that Boxer had to grab on to the bar to keep from falling. The next instant there was a tremendous explosion, followed by the roar of flames that engulfed the entire river-side of the barge.

Boxer could see several people on the *She Devil*, two, possibly three women, and at least four men. They were now aft. Two were already in the water, and two more jumped.

A woman crouched in a corner of the stern.

There was another explosion and the *She Devil* disintegrated, leaving only debris in the water, and the barge burning.

Within minutes fire trucks were on the scene, and several firemen hauled out hoses, and began wetting down the fire.

Boxer made his way out into the night, and joined the other people who had had to abandon their dinner. A mizzling rain started to fall, and right before their eyes, the barge uttered an almost human groan, and began to sink.

"I knew this would happen one day," one of the

waiters said. "That fucking boat has been playing those kinds of games for the last few weeks."

"Any idea who owned it?" Boxer asked.

"Yeah, some guy named Tony Sacco," the waiter said.

"Well, he doesn't own it now," Boxer replied. "And by the time he's finished in court, I don't think he'll own very much."

"Naw, his kind always gets away with it . . . He's got connections."

"How do you know?"

"He'd come in here a couple of nights a week. Waited on him a few times myself. He's a big tipper, but otherwise he's just scum . . . Yeah, just scum, know what I mean?"

Boxer nodded. "I know exactly what you mean."

"The guy doesn't even live here in D.C.," the waiter continued. "He's from Staten Island, wherever the hell that is."

Boxer wasn't going to give the man a geography lesson, though his mention of Staten Island rang the proverbial bell, and he remembered that it was where Gifford said he lived . . . It was something to check out when he came back—if he came back. Now, that kind of thinking, he acknowledged, was really gloomy. . . .

Boxer watched the fire fighters, now joined by a fire boat, several Coast Guard boats, and two police boats. He wondered if the people he'd seen on the *She Devil* had been rescued. But what initially had only been the diners and staff of the Barge had swelled to a huge crowd of several hundred people, including the crews from local TV stations. He wouldn't be able to get anywhere near a responsible person, who would be able to tell him anything about the people who had been rescued. He would have to find out on the eleven o'clock news.

As the rain became heavier, the crowd began to disperse. The fire was out, and the barge was nothing more than a sunken hulk, and like all sunken hulks, there wasn't the slightest hint about it of its former prettiness.

Boxer, suddenly feeling gloomier than before, had less of an appetite, and decided to return to the hotel. But before he could, he had to walk several blocks in order to find a cab.

13

Boxer skipped having dinner, left a call for 7 A.M. with the desk clerk before he went up to his room, and by ten o'clock he was in bed. Sleep came quickly, and the following morning, after a hearty breakfast of "sausages and eggs over well" and two cups of coffee, he was ready to drive down to Norfolk.

It was still raining when he slipped behind the wheel of a rented Chevy Classic, and it continued to rain during the drive down. Traffic moved slowly, and just outside of Norfolk, it came to a complete halt for several minutes because of a jack-knifed tractor trailer. But even with the half hour delay, he arrived in Norfolk at ten minutes after one in the afternoon, and was inside the navy base by half past.

The *Andrew Jackson* was moored at the end of the last quay before the dry docks began. There were other SSNs there too: the *James Monroe* and the *Alexander Hamilton*. But the *Andrew Jackson* was the largest. From bow to stern she was four hundred and fifty feet long and had a beam of seventy feet; because of the number of automated devices aboard, her crew consisted of seventy officers and sailors. She carried twenty Prosiden Two multi-warhead nuclear missiles, a variety of surface-to-air missiles for anti-aircraft defense, and eight acoustically guided high-speed torpedoes, which if necessary could be armed with nuclear charges.

Boxer crossed the gangplank, dropped his sea bag to the deck, faced the flag fluttering from a jackpole on the stern, saluted it, then turning to the duty officer, he saluted him and said, "Master Chief Jack Boxer reporting for duty, sir."

The lieutenant jg returned his salute, and checked off his name, then he said, in a southern drawl, "Welcome aboard, chief . . . Name's Hawke. Josiah Hawke. But the men call me Josh, or just Hawke." And he offered his hand.

Boxer shook it.

"Most of the other rates are aboard now, except those that are married," Hawke said, and winking broadly, he added, "Got to get that last bit in, before shipping out."

Boxer nodded vigorously and answered, "Can't ever knock that last bit, sir. It's the only bit we men have, and should always be treated with tender loving care . . . That's what makes it grow, sir."

Hawke looked at him for a moment, then started to laugh. "I think we'll get along fine, Chief . . . Just fine."

"I hope so, sir."

"Josiah, or Hawke."

"Hawke."

"Just fine," Hawke repeated.

Boxer shouldered his sea bag, and stepping across the combing, he entered the massive sail of the *Andrew Jackson*, which housed its various radar antennae, and sophisticated computers of the Underwater Imaging System that converted sonar echoes to three-dimensional images. Originally only the submarines he commanded had that equipment, but now it was standard for every boat in the fleet.

Boxer made his way down into the hull, then aft to where the rates had their quarters, and their own, albeit very small, combination lounge and rec-room.

Three men, wearing the standard work coverall, were already there. One was watching a TV talk show from an easy chair; the second was poring over the sports section of the local newspaper, and a third was studying a chessboard on which a game appeared to be in progress.

Until the moment he entered the room, Boxer hadn't any idea of how he would play the role into which he'd been cast. But it came to him as soon as he saw the three men, one of whom was also a master chief. Keeping silent, he had purposefully remained standing just inside the room. After a few seconds passed, the three men were very much aware of him. He let the silence deepen, while he moved his eyes from man to man, beginning with the MC, whose surname, he saw on the man's name tag, was Fitzhugh. The surname of the man reading the sports section was Caliendo, and the man studying the chessboard was Hicks.

Fitzhugh was a wiry, red-headed man, with icy blue eyes, and freckle-covered arms; Caliendo was black-haired and black-eyed, with a broken nose that gave him a hawkish look; and Hicks was a tall black man.

"You sure you're on the right boat?" Boxer asked, directing his question to Fitzhugh.

Fitzhugh's face reddened.

"I just gave my orders to the baby ass jg topside,"

Boxer said. "I'm supposed to be here."

"Then there'll be two of us," Fitzhugh answered, his voice low, but hard, despite its slow southern drawl.

Boxer said nothing, and flicked his eyes to Caliendo, a square-faced, chunkily built man whose "fuck you" look challenged him, then he brought his eyes to Hicks, whose eyes betrayed a smile, though he held his lips tightly together.

"Just tell me where I bunk down," Boxer said, again looking at Fitzhugh.

"Guess we'll share a compartment," Fitzhugh responded.

Boxer made a wordless sound to indicate his displeasure, and Fitzhugh answered him with, "It won't be the joy of my life either, but that's the way it will be."

"Things have a way of changin'," Boxer said, imitating Fitzhugh's drawl.

"They sure do," Fitzhugh agreed. "We got you aboard now, and ten minutes ago we didn't. That's what I call a speedy change, don't you?"

Caliendo and Hicks laughed.

"That's the best damn change you'll probably ever have on this boat," Boxer shot back, still mimicking the man's accent. "Now are you going to take me to my compartment—"

"Our compartment," Fitzhugh corrected as he stood up.

He was somewhat taller than Boxer had gauged him to have been.

"Follow me," Fitzhugh said.

Boxer stepped aside to let him pass, then to Caliendo and Hicks he said, "Pass the word to your men . . . There's a new hard ass master chief aboard . . . I don't want it to come as a surprise when they see him."

Fitzhugh stopped and said, "Either you come now, or you can fuckin' find the compartment yourself."

"I'm right behind you," Boxer said, shouldering his sea bag. "I'm right behind you."

"Yeah, that's probably where you'll always be, so you might as well get used to it," Fitzhugh said.

"We'll see about that," Boxer answered, knowing that Fitzhugh would meet him toe to toe, eyeball to eyeball, and liking him for that. Like himself, the man was a professional, and in any kind of a tight spot, he could be depended upon to give his best.

Boxer was the only rate on the bridge with commanders: Ray Johnson, the boat's skipper and Steven Walla, the EXO. He hadn't seen either the skipper or the EXO until the boat's mooring lines were about to be freed.

The EXO was taking the boat out. The forward and aft detail waited for his orders to slip the lines that were cleated to the boat.

"Slip forward line," Walla said.

Boxer lifted the bullhorn. "Slip forward line," he ordered.

The line was uncleated and heaved up on the quay, where another detail immediately began to coil it.

"Slip aft line," Walla ordered.

Boxer repeated the order to the aft detail, waited a moment, and then said, "Aft line free, sir."

Walla nodded. "Stand by to get under way," he said.

"Aye, aye, sir," Boxer replied, and called down the order to the engine room.

Moving with the outgoing tide, the boat began to drift away from the concrete quay. Overhead the sky was cloudy, and a stiff wind was blowing from the northwest. There were patches of oil on the dull gray water.

Walla checked the boat fore and aft, then he said, "All ahead, slow."

"All ahead slow," Boxer repeated, but this time he dialed the command into the engine control computer.

The single screw began to turn, and the *Jack*, as the men called her, began to gather forward momentum. Her cigar-like shape created bow waves, and a white wake.

"Come to course three-four," Walla said.

"Coming to course three-four, sir," Boxer answered, turning the master control knob on the electronic steering control.

The *Jack* answered and swung into the main channel.

"Boat clear of quay and under way," Walla reported to Johnson.

"Have the men stand muster," Johnson said.

Walla repeated the order to Boxer, who switched on the 5MC, and said, "All hands, now hear this . . . All hands, now hear this . . . All hands, now hear this . . . Report topside, afterdeck for muster . . . All hands, report topside, afterdeck for muster."

Boxer was amused. Aboard the boats he'd commanded, he had never once called the men to muster either when they had left port or when they had returned.

The men, except for those whose presence was vital to the running of the boat, assembled on the afterdeck, where the various division chiefs accounted for their men.

The skipper left the bridge to receive the report of the OD on watch. Then he put them *at ease*, and said something that Boxer couldn't hear. After he spoke, he turned the men over to the OD, and as he disappeared into the sail, the men were dismissed.

"Ahead one-third," Walla said.

"Ahead one-third, sir," Boxer answered, changing the speed control's position.

The *Jack* responded immediately. Her bow wave became bigger, and her wake deeper, whiter and longer.

They were now out in the channel, sliding by the other piers of the Norfolk Naval Base, where the carriers *America* and *Kennedy*, the battleship *New Jersey*, and several dozen guided missile cruisers, frigates, and other ships were moored.

Walla said, "We'll dive as soon as we're on the other side of the bridge."

"Yes, sir," Boxer answered, knowing that the EXO meant the Chesapeake Bay Bridge.

"About thirty minutes from now," Walla told him.

"From the way the weather is changing, it will be smoother below than topside," Boxer commented.

Walla gave him a questioning look, but didn't say anything.

They passed Tangier Island on their port side, then James Island, and when the bridge came into view, Walla asked, "How come Fitzhugh isn't on the bridge?"

"I assigned him to the control room, sir," Boxer answered. "There are two master chiefs aboard . . . Myself and Fitzhugh . . . By seniority, I outrank him."

"Oh, I wasn't aware of that," Walla said, looking at Boxer, as though he were seeing him for the first time, and taking his measure.

Boxer nodded to reaffirm what he'd just told him.

They were coming up on the bridge, and Walla now

shifted his interest from Boxer to the dive ahead. He checked with the diving officer several times to make sure there weren't any valve or pump malfunctions and that the diving planes were operational.

As they passed under the bridge, Boxer keyed himself to respond the moment Walla would order the dive.

They passed under the bridge, and almost immediately the *Jack* responded to the open expanse of the ocean that lay stretched out to the horizon, where the sea and the sky melded into a continuous sheet of dark gray.

Walla turned on the depth recorder and said, "We've got one hundred feet of water . . . One fifty . . . Stand by to dive."

Boxer switched on the 5MC. "All hands . . . All hands, stand by to dive . . . All hands, stand by to dive."

"Two hundred feet," Walla said. "Two hundred feet . . . Dive."

Boxer hit the Klaxon button, the shrill sound carried throughout the *Jack*, and then came screaming out of the open hatch just behind Boxer and Walla. "Dive . . . Dive," Boxer said over the 5MC.

The rounded bow dropped lower in the water, and in moments the forward deck was awash.

"Down sixty feet," Walla said.

Boxer moved the depth control to sixty.

Suddenly, they were struck by a deluge of cold rain.

"Secure all equipment and transfer all control to central control," Walla ordered.

Boxer repeated the command, then executed it.

The *Jack*'s hull was, now, completely underwater.

"Leave the bridge," Walla said, then as prescribed by the operation procedure, he went down the open hatch, and Boxer followed, pulling the hatch shut after him, and dogging it. Moments later, he was in the boat's control room.

The EXO had taken the Conn from the deck officer, and the *Jack,* her bow tilted slightly down, was passing through the thirty feet.

From his position just behind the DO, Boxer could see that all systems were green.

"Coming to sixty feet," the DO announced, then to the combination helmsman and planesman, he said, "On the diving planes, come zero degrees."

"Coming to sixty degrees," the operator answered.

The *Jack*'s bow came up, as the depth gauge showed she was down to sixty-five feet . . . Then, the needle moved back to sixty, and held there.

"At the mark, sixty," the DO called out, moving his eyes from the standard depth gauge to the digital depth indicator.

Walla suddenly seemed to go limp, and like a dog, shake himself, though all he moved was his head, and that only from side to side. Then he ordered a change of course, putting the boat on a southeastern tack.

Finally, he turned his attention to Boxer, and said, "I'm going to check with SUBALANTCOM about your orders."

"You're right, sir," Boxer answered. "But you'll find they are correct."

Without answering, Walla turned his attention to the instrument panel, just above the computer command console.

Boxer's experienced eyes had already checked the readings of the various dials and digital displays. Everything was normal.

Fitzhugh requested permission to enter the control

room, Walla granted it, and immediately went into a huddle with the master chief. They spoke for five minutes, then Fitzhugh left.

An hour later, the watch changed, and Fitzhugh took Boxer's place, while Boxer went aft to the chief's mess for a cup of black coffee and a freshly made whole-wheat doughnut . . . There was no doubt in his mind that even if he'd come aboard and played the role of Mister Meek, he still would have been the proverbial *odd man out* . . . "No doubt about it," he said aloud, as he finished his cup of coffee.

"Talking to yourself is the first sign," Hicks said, smiling at him.

Boxer squinted up at the black man. "'The first sign' of what?"

Hicks dropped onto the bench opposite him, and said, "All the ills that can befall a man . . . I know that whenever I start talking to myself, I'm full of self-doubt about something or other . . . And in my book, that's the worst kind of problem a man can have."

"Wrong," Boxer responded. "'The worst kind of problem a man can have' is to think he knows, or can guess, at what another man's problem is."

Hicks gave him a long, hard look and nodded. "No argument there," he said.

Boxer picked up his disposable coffee cup. "See you around," he told Hicks, and started away from the table.

"No hard feelings?"

Boxer shook his head. "That's not my game . . . See you around," he said again, and leaving the mess area, he went aft to the missile launching deck, which occupied the last third of the boat's length.

A sailor armed with a .357 magnum stopped him at the

bulkhead door, but only long enough to check that he had the necessary clearance to enter the compartment.

Inside, Boxer took the opportunity to look at the missile launch center, which was a small room manned by two officers and two enlisted men, one of whom was at least a petty officer first class. The launch center was manned twenty-four hours a day. But it could not launch a bird without the skipper and the EXO initiating the launch sequence by first activating the launch circuits with special keys, then by using their assigned, coded, personal identification number or word.

The men inside the launch center looked at Boxer; he smiled at them and pointed to the door.

One of the men opened it.

"I'm the new MC," Boxer explained. "Just looking around."

"Want to come in?"

Boxer shook his head. "But thanks, anyway."

"Anytime, Chief," the man said.

Boxer thanked him again, turned, left the missile compartment, walked a few yards forward, then down a flight of steps to the reactor compartment. There, several men were monitoring gauges and digital display devices. The power generated by the *Jack*'s reactor could push her underwater at forty knots per, and in a real pinch, probably up to forty-five knots. Like all boats, the *Jack* was faster underwater than she was on the surface. On the surface she was good for twenty knots at flank speed. But she wasn't designed to run on the surface. Her element was underwater; there she was one of the most formidable fighting machines ever created by man.

Boxer left the reactor room and worked his way through the boat to the forward torpedo room, where several different kinds of torpedoes gave the *Jack* the added capability of attacking surface vessels and other submarines. The *Jack* and her two sister boats, the *James Monroe* and the *John Paul Jones*, were designed to be two kinds of boats in one: a missile launcher and an attack submarine.

As he started back to his compartment, the 5MC came on. "Chief Boxer, report to the skipper's office immediately . . . Chief Boxer, report to the skipper's office immediately."

Boxer quickened his step, and within two minutes, he was knocking on the door of the captain's office.

"Come," Johnson called out.

Boxer entered the small office.

"Close the door," Johnson said.

Boxer obeyed, and then saluted the man. "Master Chief Jack Boxer reporting as ordered, sir," he said.

Johnson returned the salute, and gesturing to a gray metal folding chair in front of his desk, he said, "Sit down, Chief."

"Thank you, sir," Boxer responded, and settled on the chair.

"Seems like we have one chief too many," Johnson said.

Boxer didn't move or give any indication that he'd heard Johnson, who was a tall, thin man with graying brown hair and light brown eyes.

"Chief Fitzhugh has been on the *Jack* ever since I took command of her," Johnson said.

"My orders assigned me to the *Jack*, sir," Boxer told him.

Johnson picked up several pieces of paper. "They're in order, and nothing can be done to change them until we return to Norfolk. But for the duration of this cruise you will not take part in the running of this boat."

Boxer was about to object, but Johnson held up his right hand to silence him. "Master Chief Fitzhugh will continue to function as he has in the past . . . You are to consider yourself a passenger . . . Is that clear?"

"Yes, sir," Boxer answered.

"You have complete freedom of the boat, including the control room. But at no time are you to give an order that in any way affects the operation of this boat . . . Is that clear?"

"Yes, sir."

"Is there anything you want to say?" Johnson asked.

"I didn't expect to have a vacation, sir," Boxer said.

Johnson cocked his head to one side, and said, "I'm not sure how to take that."

"Any way you want to, sir," Boxer answered; he couldn't stop playing the role he'd initiated.

Johnson stared hard at him for several moments, then snapped, "Dismissed!"

Boxer stood up, came to attention, and saluted.

Johnson returned the salute.

Boxer did a precise about-face, and left the office, closing the door behind him.

14

Boxer divided his time between the control room and the *Jack's* library, which not only had several hundred books, but also a good selection of books on audio tapes, and music tapes: classical and popular.

Boxer became engrossed in a series about the navy written by Roger Jewett. The author, in a trilogy, followed the lives of four officers from the beginning of World War Two to the end of the war in Viet Nam, where the sons of the original four characters play out their individual destinies. He also listened to Hemingway's short stories: *The Short Happy Life of Francis Macomber* and *The Snows of Kilimanjaro*, which he found to be even better than he had remembered.

When he wasn't reading, or in the control room, Boxer spent time in other parts of the boat. The men, including all of the officers and Fitzhugh, were extremely courteous to him, but that didn't stop him from feeling like a non-person. It was spooky. He was there, but he really wasn't, at least not in the sense that he took part in anything with crew.

By the third day, Boxer began to get a sense of the personalities of the various men in the control room, since that was where he spent most of his time. The men were efficient, and there wasn't any doubt in his mind that Johnson ran a tight ship. Perhaps even too tight a ship. Not that he was an overzealous disciplinarian, but he was a perfectionist . . . and when something wasn't perfect, he was a screamer.

During the midwatch, at the beginning of the fourth day, Boxer, bothered by his particular situation, annoyed at himself for allowing Pierce to persuade him to become involved, and still depressed over Chuck's death, was having trouble sleeping. And rather than take a couple of sleeping pills, he left his bunk, dressed and went to the control room.

Though it was only 0130, the control room was fully operational. The *Jack*'s position, as shown on its navigation computer, was fifty miles southeast of the eastern tip of Cuba, where Johnson, who had the Conn, was playing tag with two Cuban destroyers to sharpen the crew's performance.

The destroyers were dipping and sprinting in an effort to locate the *Jack*, but Johnson, skillfully playing out various tactical situations, eluded them.

Boxer admired Johnson's skill, but because of his situation, he had to remain a shadow man and just watch, which he was doing.

"Target, bearing one five five . . . Range, eight thousand yards . . . Speed, two four knots . . . Course, seven five degrees," the sonar officer called out.

"Roger," Johnson answered. "Stand by to change course."

"Standing by to change course," the helmsman said.

"DO, come to six hundred feet," Johnson ordered.

"Making six hundred feet," the DO answered.

"Helmsman, come to new course two two five," Johnson said.

The helmsman repeated the new heading.

Boxer's attention suddenly became focused on one of the sonar operators, a gangling, blond-headed young man, named John Roberts, who was a petty officer third class. There was something about the expression on the man's face that fixed Boxer's attention on it. There was an overall tightness about it, especially around the lips. Roberts was looking at the amber-colored sonar display, and seemed to Boxer to be transfixed by it. Boxer had seen the same thing happen several times before. The moving light on the sonar display, or radar, had actually hypnotized the man.

Hicks was the nearest man to Roberts, and Boxer was about to call his attention to the situation, when suddenly the young man removed his headphones and slowly stood up.

Hicks saw him.

Then Roberts shouted, "This is God's boat, and I am his instrument."

Johnson whirled around.

Roberts reached down under the sonar console, and pulled out an Uzi . . . The next instant he began firing: first at Johnson, then at Hicks, and finally at the OD.

Johnson took a burst in his chest. Half of Hicks's head came off. The OD came apart at his knees.

In less than five seconds the deck was splashed with blood.

"Targets, closing fast," the SO reported, his voice tight with fear.

"No one move," Roberts said, waving the Uzi back and forth. "I will take this boat and sail it into God's harbor."

No one moved.

"Surface," Roberts ordered. "Surface, and we'll sail into the harbor of the Lord."

The EXO, Fitzhugh, and several junior officers came running into the control room, and were cut down by three more quick bursts.

"Surface!" Roberts shouted.

"We'll come up in front—"

The man squeezed off a short burst.

The diving officer's face dissolved into a bloody pulp.

Boxer suddenly moved into the center of the control room and shouted, "Lo, I have seen the instrument of God, and his name is Roberts, and he is the captain of this ship and will sail us into God's own harbor."

Confused, Roberts looked at him.

"The Lord wants this boat in his harbor," Boxer shouted, moving closer to Roberts. "He wants this boat—"

"Targets—" the SO began.

"The Lord sees all, isn't that right, Roberts?" Boxer asked.

"Yes."

"The Lord put me here to help you," Boxer said. He was now very close to Roberts. "He brought me here to help you."

"Surface!" Roberts shouted.

But the next instant the Cuban sonar pinged through the boat.

Boxer began to sweat. The Cubans were ranging on the *Jack*, and though they were using old Russian sonar equipment and would soon fire equally old ASROCS, or drop ash cans, they still could severely damage the boat, or, worse, send it to the bottom . . . and the bottom here was almost two miles down.

"Ash cans, on the way down," the SO reported.

Boxer reached Roberts, and even as their eyes met, his right hand came up, and caught the man on the right side of his head.

Roberts started to fall, and Boxer wrenched the Uzi from him, then drove his knee into the man's groin. "Secure him," he ordered.

Two other sonar men grabbed Roberts and pinioned his arms.

"Get him the fuck out of here," Boxer told them; then moving to the control console he dialed in flank speed.

The Cuban sonar was still pinging off on the *Jack*.

"Maximum depth, crash dive!" Boxer ordered.

"Making maximum depth," the stunned DO repeated.

"Helmsman, come to three hundred degrees," Boxer said, while he checked the water temperature digital display.

"Three hundred degrees," the helmsman answered.

Suddenly two huge explosions burst above and on the *Jack*'s starboard side, rolling her violently to her port side . . . Moments later she rolled to the starboard, then to the port . . . Finally she came to a normal position.

Boxer got on the 5MC. "Report any damage to the control room," he ordered.

Two more explosions slammed down on the *Jack*, one on the forward deck, and the other above the sail.

"Helmsman, come to ninety degrees," Boxer ordered, his eyes looking at the water temperature readout again. The *Jack* was moving into colder water. The temperature differential between the two layers would shield the *Jack* from the Cuban sonar.

"Coming to ninety degrees," the helmsman responded.

Suddenly Hawke and two other officers came into the control room and stopped dead in their tracks when they saw the bloody bodies on the deck.

"Taking evasive action," Boxer said, just as the pinging from the Cuban sonar stopped, then with a sigh of relief he added, "The *Jack* is secure, sirs."

"But how could you have—" one of the officers began to ask.

"Sir, I just did it," Boxer answered. "Now, if you'll excuse me—"

"We'll need a full report," Hawke said.

"Yes, sir," Boxer answered, then he added, "Everything was taped."

"We'll still need statements from every man in the control room," Hawke insisted.

"Yes, sir," Boxer repeated, saluted the officers, and left the control room.

The *Jack* returned to Norfolk, and just two hours after she tied up, Boxer was in Washington, seated across from Pierce, explaining what had happened.

"Seems that Roberts was an alcoholic," Pierce said. "But somehow his condition— Well, no one thought it serious enough to recommend treatment and removal from duty until the problem was under control."

Boxer fished out his pipe, filled it, and lit it before he said, "That oversight cost the lives of half a dozen good men, and might have cost the lives of every one of us aboard the *Jack*." He blew a cloud of smoke into the air. "The Cubans were hot on our tail . . . It could have well been a disaster."

"But it wasn't, thanks to you," Pierce said.

Boxer didn't answer.

"Why don't you take a few days off, then we'll talk," Pierce told him.

"There's nothing to talk about," Boxer said. "I don't want to become involved in anything remotely resembling the kind of assignment I just had . . . No thank you . . . I'll do what I said I would do."

"And what was that?"

"Buy a schooner, or some kind of a sailboat, and—"

"Listen, Jack, that kind of thing is long gone," Pierce told him.

"Not for me, it isn't . . . That kind of thing is what my dreams are made of," Boxer told him.

Pierce shook his head. "Kahn is going to go after your ass."

"At least I'll know who is after it . . . I don't appreciate being a non-person, and that was what I was . . . You can tell Kahn that I'm not going to play any more of his clandestine agents for him, or for anyone else. Now, I just want to live and let live. I've had enough."

"That's about as long a speech as I've ever heard from you," Pierce said.

Boxer blew more smoke out, stood up, and walked to the window. The CNO's office had a lovely view of the Virginia countryside, which now rested under an autumnal gray sky.

"Christ, Sam," Boxer began, taking the liberty of not only using his given name, but also shortening it, "don't you ever want something else . . . something different from all of this?"

"Certainly . . . I'm going to retire in two years and raise miniature horses," Pierce answered.

Boxer turned and looked at him.

"I'm not joking . . . There's one hell of a market for them, especially with the rich Japanese and Koreans."

"Miniature horses," Boxer commented, not knowing what else to say.

"I actually have started . . . I have some sixty acres on the Eastern Shore, and half a dozen horses. Two stallions and four brood mares."

Boxer walked back to the chair and sat down again. "Understand, I'm tired . . . I don't want to fight Kahn, or anyone else."

Pierce cut the end off a cigar, and lit it. "Give yourself some time before you make your final decision . . . A few months, at least!"

"I don't need a few months," Boxer answered.

"Then do it for me," Pierce said. "I just want you to be sure that what you do will be what you want to do."

"All right, I'll take the time."

Pierce nodded, then he asked, "What are you going to do now—I mean in the immediate future . . . The next few days?"

"Not much of anything," Boxer said. "I was thinking of going up to New York, and spend some time there; then I'll probably be with Stark for awhile . . . We're going to start looking for a boat."

"The two of you are going to sail it?" Pierce asked.

"And anyone else who wants to join us."

"How big a boat are you thinking about buying?"

"At least large enough to sleep six comfortably, and, if the price is right, more," Boxer answered.

Pierce reached across the desk, shook Boxer's hand and wished him luck.

"I'll be in touch," Boxer said, getting to his feet and

saluting his superior.

Smiling, Pierce returned the salute.

Boxer left the CNO's office, went down to the lobby, found a public phone, and called Stark.

"You're not supposed to be back," Stark said.

"I'll tell you about it when I see you," Boxer replied.

"When will that be?"

"I'm going up to New York for a few days," Boxer said. "I have some legal matters to attend to, and I think a few days up there might do me some good."

Stark was silent.

"There are some places I want to see," Boxer explained. "Hell, I have this need to just go there, and look at some of the places where I spent my youth."

Stark uttered a wordless grunt of disdain. "Never helps to go back, and have a look see . . . It's never the same . . . Hell, you aren't the same."

Boxer wasn't about to try to change Stark's viewpoint, and even if he tried, he couldn't. Besides, Stark was probably right. But that didn't change what he intended to do.

"I'll see you in a few days," Boxer said. "I'll call before I come down."

"If you don't get me, leave a message on the tape," Stark answered.

"You have an answering machine?" Boxer questioned. Stark had vowed he would never get one.

"Just keeping up with the times," Stark answered.

"Next thing you'll get is a mobile phone," Boxer teased.

"I've been thinking about it," Stark said.

"My, my, I'm away a few days, and—"

"How are you?" Stark asked, interrupting him.

"I'm fine," Boxer answered. "But I'm tired . . . No, I'm very tired."

"You sound it," Stark said. "Do what you have to do in New York, then you get your ass down here, and just relax."

"See you in a few days," Boxer said.

"See you," Stark responded.

Boxer listened to the click on the other end before he put the phone back in its cradle. For a moment, he remained seated in the telephone booth . . . Now, with the exception of Borodine, Stark was the only person he had any real ties to. Everyone else was dead . . . Boxer pursed his lips . . . Feeling sorry for himself wasn't going to change a damn thing. It would only make him more depressed, and he could do without that . . . Boxer left the phone booth, and with as jaunty a stride as he could manage, he walked through the corridor and followed the blue markers to the parking lot.

15

The following morning, despite the rain, Boxer shuttled up to New York, then cabbed into Manhattan, where he checked in at the Plaza Hotel. By afternoon, the rain stopped, and Boxer took the opportunity to walk down Fifth Avenue.

The stores were nowhere as elegant as he'd remembered them. Though he was dressed in blue jeans, and a blue hooded navy sweatshirt, and a short all-weather jacket, he stopped in Saks to browse in the men's department.

A gray-haired salesman immediately came up to him. "Is there anything in particular that you are looking for?" the man asked, with just a hint of a sneer in his voice.

"Just looking," Boxer answered, aware that the man viewed him as a potential shoplifter.

The man nodded, moved away, but kept his eyes on him.

Boxer stopped at a tie display, where the hand-painted silk ties sold for a hundred dollars apiece.

"Those are very expensive," the salesman said,

coming up behind Boxer.

"I hadn't noticed," Boxer answered.

"Each one is an original," the salesman said.

"An original what?"

The man gave him a questioning look, and before he could speak, Boxer said, "I'll take all of them."

"What?"

"You just sold me twelve ties," Boxer said with a straight face, and taking out his American Express card, he added, "Have them sent this afternoon by special messenger to Admiral Jack Boxer, care of the Plaza Hotel."

"You're—"

"I am. Now, if you'd take care of the paperwork—"

"Certainly, sir," the man said, nodding, and at the same time smiling obsequiously.

In a matter of moments, Boxer scrawled his name on the charge slip and handed it back to the salesman.

"We have some very fine shirts," the man said.

Boxer shook his head. "I didn't even need the ties," he answered, then did a precise about-face and walked away. He didn't have to look back to know the man's face was very red.

As soon as he was back on the street, Boxer crossed Fifth Avenue to Rockefeller Center and continued to walk south. The number of schlock shops amazed and depressed him. But he continued to walk.

By the time Boxer reached Twenty-Eighth Street, he realized he was hungry and that he really wasn't enjoying himself. He recrossed Fifth Avenue and headed east, hoping to find a restaurant where he could have lunch and relax.

Halfway between Lexington and Third Avenues, he saw the Purple Cow, a restaurant that he had read about in some magazine that featured New York eateries. He remembered that the place catered to the city's book publishing set. It was a place editors, writers and their agents frequented. And the article said that on any given day there was likely to be at least one luminary from the world of publishing lunching there. The writer also stated that the food was excellent, though somewhat pricey.

Boxer decided to lunch there. He walked down the three steps, entered, and found himself in a small vestibule, painted white, decorated with copper pots and spoons.

An actorish young man, with blond hair and an open-necked shirt that revealed his almost hairless chest, immediately confronted Boxer, and in a very theatrical voice, he asked, "Do you have a reservation?"

Boxer almost burst into laughter . . . First the salesman in Saks, now this . . . this would-be Hamlet . . .

"There is at least a two-hour wait," the maitre d' said, his blue eyes fastened on Boxer.

Boxer leaned slightly forward. "Is there really?" he responded.

"Absolutely."

Boxer said in a whisper, "You don't recognize me, do you?" He was beginning to enjoy himself.

The young man looked at him quizzically. "Should I—"

Boxer smiled and named a famous author of suspense novels. "I just thought that—"

"Certainly, Mr.—"

Boxer put his forefinger against his lips. "Please, I'd like a little privacy."

"Certainly, I understand," the maitre d' answered.

"If, for any reason, you must address me, you may call me Admiral Boxer."

"Admiral Boxer?"

"The name of one of my new characters," Boxer said.

"Will you follow me, Admiral?" the young man said, picking up a gigantic menu bound in red leather, and decorated with the imprint of a purple cow on the front and a yellow tassel on the bottom.

Boxer finally was ensconced on a wicker-backed chair at a table that overlooked a garden, now filled with autumnal dreariness, and made even drearier by the drizzle that had begun to fall.

Boxer ordered a Stoli on the rocks, and looked around. The decor was colonial American, but it wouldn't have passed for anything more than a cheap imitation in Williamsburg, Virginia. But it did give the room a certain ambience, which was greatly enhanced by a huge fieldstone fireplace, with a real fire going in it, not more than a dozen paces from where he sat.

Opening the large menu, Boxer was surprised to find that it was done calligraphically, probably on parchment, he guessed. He began to give it the serious study it deserved, if for no other reason than it was pretty to look at in its own right. Eventually, after he'd just about finished drinking his Stoli, he found himself vacillating between a beef pie, with garden fresh vegetables, and veal cordon bleu with linguini and butter sauce, mushrooms, and shallots. He was just about to choose the beef pie when he heard his name called by a woman.

Boxer made a half turn to his right.

"I was sure it was you," Toni-Ann said, coming up to him and kissing him on his lips before he had a chance to stand. "What are you doing here? And why didn't you—"

Boxer finally got to his feet.

"Are you with anyone?" Toni-Ann asked.

"No."

"I'm with some people over there." She gestured toward a table where three women and two men were staring at him.

Suddenly, she took hold of his forearms and said, "Let me look at you . . . What happened? You look terrible."

"It's a long and boring story," he answered.

"Are you in the city alone?" she asked.

Boxer nodded.

"For how long?"

"No specific amount of time," Boxer answered, now aware of the musky scent of her perfume and that she was wearing a dark green suit and a white blouse with a plunging neckline. "For a few days, or until I get rid of this need to go back to my roots."

"You'd be the last one I'd guess who'd get into the nostalgic bit," she said.

"You'd be surprised what I could get into," he answered, looking directly into her blue eyes.

"Yes, I know what you can get into," she said.

For a moment, neither one of them spoke, and Boxer wanted to sweep her into his arms and ask her to go back to the hotel with him.

"I have to go back to my table," she said. "Those three women are editors at the magazine."

"And the men?"

"The beefy one is an illustrator, and the other one is a writer," she explained.

"I told the maitre d' I was Robert Ludlum," Boxer said.

She started to laugh. "And he believed you?"

"I also told him to call me Admiral Boxer."

"You didn't, did you?"

Boxer nodded.

"I have to go," Toni-Ann said.

Boxer glanced over at the table and commented, "They look as if they're getting impatient."

"Call me," Toni-Ann said. "Please."

"Where?"

"At home . . . I'm listed in the phone book. I live on York Avenue."

"I'll call," Boxer said.

"Where are you staying?" she asked.

"The Plaza . . . Why?"

"If you don't call me, I'll call you," Toni-Ann said, and leaning forward, kissed him on the lips, opened her mouth, and flicked her tongue against his. Then, smiling at him, she turned around and hurried back to her table.

Savoring the taste of her lips, Boxer sat down, and remembered how delicious the intimate parts of her body tasted.

By the time Boxer finished his lunch, the rain had stopped, but it remained bleak, and though there wasn't any way for him to really know until he was outside again, it looked as if it had turned colder.

Throughout lunch, Boxer scrupulously had avoided looking at Toni-Ann, and when she and her party left, he exchanged only the most imperceptible of nods . . . Someone would have had to be looking hard at them to have seen it. . . .

He paid the check, left a large tip for the waiter, and, on his way out, Boxer also tipped the blond maitre d'. As soon as he was out on the street, he was aware that his guess had been right: the temperature had dropped sharply, and a cutting wind blew from west to east.

Boxer had planned to use the remainder of the afternoon for a trip into Brooklyn, to visit where he had been born and spent the first twelve years of his life, before his father had bought a house on Staten Island. His plan had been to go back to the old neighborhood by subway, but the cold and the feeling of weariness undercut his resolve. He would go to Brooklyn the following day. Now, all he really wanted to do was to go back to the hotel and nap. He walked to Third Avenue, hailed the first empty cab he saw, and settling down in the back, he told the driver to take him to the Plaza Hotel.

Because of various construction jobs, including the laying of new water mains, traffic crawled, and the almost constant honking of dozens of horns not only made it seem to move slower, but it also gave him a headache.

His driver, with the unlikely name of Adnon Rieman, was a small, dark-complexioned man with a black mustache and black flashing eyes, who could have passed for a member of the Palestine Liberation Organization. But here he was driving a cab in New York City. Years ago, when he was growing up in the city, the driver's counterpart would have been a Jew, or an Italian, sometimes even an Irishman. . . .

Even as these thoughts slipped through his mind, Boxer heard the crash of metal striking metal and was bounced across the back seat of the cab.

The driver stopped and rushed out of the cab.

Boxer pulled himself into a sitting position. He wasn't hurt, but he had been violently jarred. Aware that the cab and the other car were now just another obstacle for other vehicles, Boxer would have much preferred the driver to pull over to the side to continue his argument with the other driver, a young, dark-haired man, whose white Mustang's right side was totally crushed.

"But you hit me," Boxer heard the cab driver shout. "You hit me . . . I saw you cutting from one lane to the other in my rearview mirror."

"I don't give a fuck about your rearview mirror," the man answered.

"Let me have your license and your insurance card," the cabbie said.

"Fuck you, man!" the young man answered. "You ain't gettin' nothin' from me."

Boxer opened the door of the cab and got out.

"This ain't any of your fuckin' business," the young man shouted at Boxer and pushed the cabbie in the chest.

"Someone call a cop," the cabbie yelled to the people, who now ringed the two vehicles to see what was happening.

"I ain't waitin' here," the young man yelled. "You fuckin' want me, you're goin' to fuckin' have to find me."

"That's not the way it's going to be," Boxer said in a quiet but angry voice.

"What?" the young man shouted, then challenged, "And you're goin' to stop me?" He reached inside his car and pulled out a lug wrench. "Come on, you son of a bitch," he said, waving his free hand toward himself. "Come on, an' just try it." He was in his early twenties, dark-complexioned, and he wore a fleece-lined rancher's coat, tooled cowboy boots, and several gold chains around his neck.

"Go get 'im, Vinny," a woman yelled from inside the car.

Boxer picked up on his name. "Mistake, Vinny," he said flatly. With his blood now pounding in his ears, he suddenly did a side leap. His right foot struck Vinny in the chest, throwing him against the side of the car, then he grabbed the lug wrench out of Vinny's hand, and dropped it to the ground. Finally, Boxer landed a right cross, followed by a left hook that bloodied the young man's nose.

A cop finally arrived, and Boxer told him what had happened.

Vinny, bleeding from the nose and from his lower lip, and with a spike-haired woman by his side, pointed his finger at Boxer. "You're fuckin' dead, mister . . . Fuckin' dead." Then turning to the cop, he said, "I'm Vinny Marcco . . . You know Marcco?"

The cop hesitated.

"You tell these two fucks that—"

"Arrest him," Boxer said.

"What? You're goin'—"

"Either you arrest him, now, officer, or I will arrest him, and then have you up for dereliction of duty," Boxer said, now very angry.

"Just who the fuck do you think you are?" Vinny asked. "He ain't goin' to arrest me."

Boxer dug into his back trouser pocket, pulled out his wallet, opened it, and showed his ID to the cop.

"Admiral Boxer?" the cop questioned.

"That's right . . . Now I can, as a federal agent, arrest him," Boxer said. "But if I do it—"

The cop got on his radio and called for backup, then he said to Vinny, "Okay, turn around, palms on the car, and assume the position."

"You're—"

"Do it!" the cop ordered.

In less than five minutes, a squad car arrived, and Vinny Marcco was cuffed and on his way to Manhattan North, the police station on Forty-ninth Street, off Eighth Avenue.

"I'll talk to your captain, as soon as I reach my hotel," Boxer said. "The punk is going to get some time for this."

"I wouldn't be so sure about it," the cop answered. "His father has a lot of connections."

Boxer smiled. "I have a few myself." Then he thanked the cop and started to get back in the cab.

"Hey, Admiral, what about me?" the young woman asked, whose name, Boxer had learned, when she had stated it to the police, was Lorraine Giadonno.

Boxer took a good look at her. She probably was in her early twenties. She was attractive, maybe even beautiful. But it wouldn't last. By the time she was thirty, she would probably be heavy-featured and have trouble keeping her weight down.

"What about me?' she whined.

Boxer gave her a ten-dollar bill, and told her to take a cab home.

"And that's it?" Lorraine asked.

"That's it," Boxer answered.

"Vinny is such a jerk," she commented. "I told him not to cut in and out. I told him that he was going to hit another car."

Boxer shrugged.

"What about Vinny's car?" she questioned.

"I couldn't care less about Vinny's car," Boxer said, and finally settling down on the rear seat of Adnon's cab, he told him to drive to the hotel.

16

By the time he reached the hotel, Boxer's nerves were frayed, and to put himself in a more mellow mood, he stopped in the cocktail lounge for a drink, and seating himself at the bar he ordered another Stoli on the rocks.

Except for his unexpected meeting with Toni-Ann, Boxer wasn't in the least bit pleased with his visit to New York, and was beginning to think that, maybe, it wasn't a good idea for him to indulge himself by following the nostalgia route . . . maybe, he was one of the few who should not try to go back . . . But then his thoughts switched to Toni-Ann, and immediately ignition took place in his groin. He wanted her, and it was obvious that she wanted him too.

Boxer put his empty glass down, when the barkeep, at the end of the bar, called out, "Is Admiral Boxer here?"

"Yes," Boxer answered.

"Call, sir," the barkeep said. "You can either take it in the booth over there," the man said, gesturing toward the side where there were four phone booths, "or on the portable phone."

"The booth," Boxer answered, leaving the stool. He made his way across the room to the first booth, sat down, and, as he picked up the phone, he closed the door.

"This is Mr. Marcco," the voice on the other end said.

"I don't think we have anything to discuss," Boxer told him.

"My son—"

"You interrupted my quiet time," Boxer said, cutting Marcco short. "Now, if you'll excuse me, or even if you won't, I'll go back to it." He hung up and returned to the bar where he finished his drink before he went up to his suite on the fortieth floor.

Boxer took off his jacket and hooded sweatshirt, walked to the window, and looked down at Central Park. The rain had started again, and this time it was heavier.

He left the window, walked into the bedroom, and stretched out on the king-sized bed. He reached over to the phone on the night table, and called information for the number of the magazine where Toni-Ann worked. Then he punched it out, and Toni-Ann's assistant answered, who told him that Toni-Ann had already left for the day.

Boxer called information again, and this time he asked for Toni-Ann's home phone. He punched that number into the phone. After three rings, her answering machine came on. He was about to hang up, but decided not to. Instead, he left his name, rank, and serial number, and told her to call him. Then he put the phone down, closed his eyes, and drifted off to sleep.

Kahn was livid. "And you just let Boxer go?" he hissed

at Pierce. "You just let him walk out of your office?"

"The man needs a rest," Pierce said, lighting a cigar and blowing the smoke to one side.

"You don't seem to understand that he hasn't completed his mission," Kahn said.

Pierce shook his head. "It seems to me that you don't seem to understand that Jack Boxer saved the *Andrew Jackson* and her crew from—"

"He's your fucking hero, not mine," Kahn growled.

"You're right about that," Pierce said.

"Get his ass back here, now!"

"No way," Pierce answered, blowing another cloud of smoke toward the ceiling, but this time managing to send some of it across the desk at Kahn.

"That's not funny," Kahn responded, while coughing. "Not funny at all."

"It wasn't meant to be," Pierce told him.

"All right, I'll give him two weeks," Kahn said. "Then, if he's not back here, I will take the appropriate action."

"Let me guess what that will be . . . Ah, you'll fire him."

"Don't joke, Admiral."

"I'm not joking . . . I think that Jack would make you regret that."

"Is that a threat, or rather, did he make that threat?" Kahn asked.

"No . . . But just for your own peace of mind, or more to the point, so that you don't get any strange ideas about Boxer."

"I'm listening."

"He has as much political clout as the President has, certainly more than you have, only he doesn't use it . . .

I wouldn't be stupid enough to make him use it."

Kahn nodded. "Is that a fact?"

"It's a fact," Pierce answered.

"I'll try to remember it," Kahn said, getting to his feet. "I'll try real hard, unless Boxer is stupid enough to make me forget it . . . Tell him what I said." He turned and went to the door.

"Kahn," Pierce called, and when the Company director stopped and faced him, he pointed the cigar at him, and said, "You push Boxer hard enough, and you just might find yourself out of a job, or worse, dead . . . Boxer's men are loyal to him, and wouldn't enjoy seeing their skipper hurt."

"Now, that is a threat, isn't it?" Kahn said with obvious relish.

"It's the way things are," Pierce said.

Kahn nodded, turned around and walked out of the room.

"Jackass," Pierce muttered after him. "A jackass, if there ever was one!"

The ringing sound of the phone mutated into the scream of the Klaxon, taking Boxer into an obscure memory of something having gone wrong aboard a submarine under his command . . . He thrashed around on the bed . . . *Damage control, report . . . Stand by, all hands, stand by . . . Fire in forward torpedo room . . . Dive . . . Dive . . . Dive.*

Boxer couldn't breathe. He wrenched himself out of his sleep. The phone was still ringing. The room was pitch black, except for the light that filtered through the window. Still, vexed by the dream and drenched with sweat, Boxer picked up the phone, cleared his throat, and said, "Boxer here!"

"Good God, I've been trying to get you for the last three hours," Toni-Ann sang. "Where have you been?"

He cleared his throat again. "Here, sleeping."

"You never heard—"

"What time is it?" Boxer asked.

"Going on ten o'clock."

With his free hand, Boxer rubbed his forehead. "I guess I was tired."

"Too tired to have a visitor?" she asked. "I could be there in half an hour, less if I am able to find a cab quickly."

"I'll order up something to eat," Boxer said, realizing he was hungry.

"You mean you haven't had dinner yet?"

"I told you I was sleeping."

"Listen, we're wasting time. I'm coming over. See you soon," she said, then the line went dead.

Boxer put the phone back on the night table, when suddenly he smelled smoke, cigarette smoke. He remembered he had been dreaming about a fire in the forward torpedo room. "Christ, it was no damn dream," he muttered, and started to stand, only to discover that his legs were tied.

"He's up," a man announced.

The lights were switched on, and Boxer found himself looking at Gifford and that punk he had tangled with earlier.

"Nothing to say, Admiral?" the man, whom he had known as Gifford, asked.

"Marcco?"

"That's my real name . . . Gifford is one of the ones I use when I travel."

Boxer looked down at his bound legs.

"Just a precaution," Marcco said. "My son told me how well you use them."

Boxer said nothing.

"Aren't you going to ask any questions?" Marcco asked.

"You'll give me the answers without me asking the questions," Boxer said.

Marcco nodded, turned to Vinny and said, "Here's a lesson for you . . . Even now he can keep his mouth shut, and that's something you still don't know how to do."

Boxer pulled himself up and leaned against the bed's headboard. "There's a pipe and tobacco in my jacket pocket," he said.

"Get the man his pipe and tobacco," Marcco told his son.

"I'd like to get my hands on that fucker," Vinny answered.

"Do like I said," Marcco ordered, "or I'll make you fucking wish you were never born."

Vinny dug out the pipe and tobacco pouch from Boxer's jacket.

"There's a lighter there too," Boxer said.

"No lighter," Marcco snapped. "You want to light up, Vinny will hold the lighter for you . . . Won't you, Vin?"

"Sure, sure . . . Anything you say."

Marcco smiled, or at least his lips stretched and parted in a pretense of a smile. Then he said, "Vinny is like his mom, spoiled rotten . . . Always got everything he wanted, and more . . . Kids today have no ambition. They just want to run wild."

Boxer answered, "That's one kid who should have a few lessons on how to behave."

Marcco nodded. "He thinks he's a big fuckin' man because he can throw my name around, and drive a new fuckin' car, and fucks an eighteen-year-old bitch—"

"Pa—" Vinny began.

But his father waved him silent. "I don't want to hear nothin' from you . . . You cost me ten Gs tonight, and probably a fuck of a lot more."

Boxer finished filling the pipe bowl and said to Vinny, "Light, please."

Marcco smacked his son on top of the head. "Listen, did you hear what the admiral said . . . He said 'please,' that's what he fuckin' said. Even in this situation, the man is polite. You can learn a lot from him, and you're going to. By all the fuckin' saints, you're going to learn how to keep your ass out of trouble."

Vinny leaned close to Boxer, flicked on the cigarette lighter, and held it over the pipe's bowl. "Get it done fast," he said, through clenched teeth. Then he whispered, "What goes around comes around. I got a score to settle with you."

"What are you saying?" Marcco wanted to know.

"He's just telling me what a pleasure it is for him to be here," Boxer said, while still lighting the pipe.

"Yeah, I bet," Marcco responded.

Vinny moved away from the column of smoke that came out of Boxer's pipe.

"As soon as your lady friend gets here," Marcco said, "we'll be on our way."

Boxer still didn't ask any questions or make a comment. He had already realized that one of them had listened to his conversation with Toni-Ann, and knew that she was on her way there. He'd also come to the conclusion that he wasn't going to be *worked over*, at least not for the time being.

"You know," Marcco said, "when I first met you, and found out who you were, I said to myself that we'd meet sometime in the future."

"I can't say I felt the same way," Boxer replied, suddenly realizing that he'd never pressed Pierce to find out if there was a connection between Marcco—then known as Gifford—and Kahn.

Suddenly there was a knock at the door.

"Your lady friend," Marcco said, and going over to Boxer, he cut the bonds around his legs. "You let her in . . . Any play on your part, you're dead, and so is she. Understand?"

Boxer nodded, stood up, and went to the door.

"Open it," Marcco said in a loud whisper.

Boxer glanced over his left shoulder.

The two thugs Marcco had with him had their .375s trained on him.

Boxer faced the door and opened it.

Toni-Ann threw herself against Boxer.

He held her tightly. "Don't be frightened," he whispered.

"Why should I—"

"Close the door, Admiral," Marcco ordered.

Boxer eased Toni-Ann away from him, and led her inside, then he closed the door.

"Weren't you at the Hawksbill—"

"Yes, I was there."

"What a broad!" Vinny exclaimed. "Look at her—"

"Shut up!" his father snapped. Then to Toni-Ann, "He thinks with his cock."

"What's going on?" Toni-Ann questioned, looking at Boxer, and obviously frightened.

Marcco answered, "What's going on is that the admiral and my son got into a scrape, and my son came out the worse for it . . . And it cost me ten Gs to get him out of the hands of the police, and so it's payback time."

"Do you know what he's talking about?" Toni-Ann asked.

Boxer was about to answer, when Marcco said, "It's easy . . . I don't need his money, I need what he knows how to do . . . He's going to bring a submarine—"

"What?" Boxer exploded.

"Ah, that got a rise out of you, didn't it, Admiral," Marcco laughed. He looked at Vinny and said, "I bet he has it all figured out without me telling him a thing . . . That's because he uses his brains. Brains, Vinny; that's what it takes to be someone in this fuckin' world. You can pump iron all you want, but it don't mean a fuckin' thing unless you got your brain all pumped up too."

Boxer put his right arm around Toni-Ann's shoulders. "She hasn't anything to do—"

"She's my insurance," Marcco said, smiling. "She and your friend Stark."

Boxer pulled his arm free.

"Easy, Admiral, I don't want to hurt your lady friend," Marcco said. "I don't want to have my friends take her into the next room, and—"

Boxer's cheeks burned.

"All you have to do," Marcco said, "is make one run, and the three of you will be let go, and with enough money to make you happy for a long, long time."

"You have a boat?" Boxer asked.

"Yeah, I call it Marcco's Navy," he laughed.

Vinny and the two thugs laughed too.

"Nothing fancy," Marcco said. "A World War Two Tango class, nothin' as fancy as the kind of boat you're used to. But it will get the job done."

"That's what was out of sight the night you were on the beach," Boxer said.

"That's what was out there," Marcco answered. "But the skipper got greedy, and you know that being greedy causes problems."

Boxer didn't answer.

"The boat has sonar, and it can get the job done," Marcco said.

"And if I say I won't do it?" Boxer questioned.

"Then you and your two friends are dead, but before she dies, well—"

"This is some kind of joke, isn't it?" Toni-Ann asked, her voice rising in pitch.

Boxer took hold of her arm. "It's not a joke," he said.

"Now, let me explain . . . So you don't pull any tricks: your lady friend and your old buddy are going to be on the boat with you, and so is Vinny, and a couple of my men."

"What about the crew?"

"There's an even dozen . . . Just enough to operate the boat. This ain't no wartime patrol . . . All they gotta do is make it go down, run it when it's down, then make it come up, and run it when it's on the surface. Simple."

Boxer didn't answer.

"Okay, we leave the hotel through the basement . . . There are cars waiting for us. We should be at the boat by dawn."

"Where is the boat?"

Marcco waved a finger at him. "And I thought you wouldn't ask any questions."

"See, Pa, you got him worried," Vinny said.

"Don't you kid yourself; guys like Boxer never worry," Marcco said, then he started to laugh.

17

As soon as Boxer and Toni-Ann were in one of the two limousines that were waiting on the street, they were quickly blindfolded. Then, after about an hour of driving, the limos stopped, their blindfolds were removed, they were led out to a ten-passenger helicopter, and within a matter of moments they were airborne.

Boxer could tell from the position of the Big Dipper that they were heading south, and because they were flying very low, he could see the coast and some of the large cities along it.

He guessed they were doing about a hundred miles an hour, tops a hundred and twenty-five. There were hundreds, maybe even thousands of places along the coast where a submarine could be hidden. The trick would be to keep it hidden from the locals, but even that could be compensated for by choosing one of the more remote inlets. But the real trick would be to move it undetected out to sea, then back again. Once at sea, the problem of detection would be minimized. It could stay below during the daylight hours, just the way it had during World War Two, and then, as soon as darkness came, it would surface to charge its batteries. Because it was a stripped-down version of the Tango class boats, Boxer figured its tonnage was less, and therefore it could spend more time at sea.

Through most of the flight, Marcco slept, but Vinny couldn't seem to settle down. Finally, he woke his father and said, "I ain't goin' on the fuckin' submarine."

For the better part of three seconds, Marcco looked confused. Then the words his son had just spoken must have sunk in, and he reacted by backhanding Vinny across the face. "Listen, you fuck, you're goin' to do what I tell you, or I'll throw you out of the fuckin' door, now!"

Vinny cowered in his seat.

Marcco pointed to him. "Never had any fuckin' guts," he said. "Just wind, and fuckin' gold chains."

Vinny looked at Boxer. "How far down will it go?" he asked.

Boxer shrugged . . . The boy was spooked. He could spook him more, and maybe that would help him get Stark and Toni-Ann out of this. "Boat can operate at four hundred and seventy-five feet; take it lower and the plates begin to scream, then the rivets begin to pop. Take it lower—you might never be able to surface again."

Vinny was visibly shaken.

"But nothin' is gonna happen to you," Marcco said. "Because the admiral wants to keep himself and his two friends alive." Then he looked at Boxer. "Sometimes a father has to take the hard way to teach his son how to be a man."

Boxer didn't answer.

"I ain't goin'," Vinny whimpered.

Marcco mimicked his son, then uttered a gigantically loud sigh, placed his head back on the seat's headrest, and closed his eyes.

Boxer wondered what kind of thoughts Marcco might be having. He certainly couldn't be proud of his son, and as for anything else—well, it probably would take several well-trained psychiatrists to even begin to figure out Marcco's thought processes, such as they were.

He leaned over to Toni-Ann, who seemed paralyzed with fear, and, forcing a playful tone, he whispered, "I guess it doesn't pay to visit strange men in their hotel rooms at night."

"I think you're actually enjoying this," she came back at him.

"Not in the least . . . I'm as frightened as you are, maybe more, because I know all of the things that can happen."

She was quiet for a moment, then she said urgently, "We have to do something."

"Certainly, we have to do something, but not now."

"When?"

"When we can be sure it will pay off," Boxer answered. "Now, the only thing we can do—must do—is go along with what they want."

Toni-Ann didn't respond, and Boxer could see that she didn't like what he'd said, so he added, "The shark was easy by comparison. These men, especially Marcco, have brains, and out only chance to get out of this alive is to outthink them."

"You think Marcco is going to kill us?" she asked, her face going absolutely white.

"Not now . . . Later, when we've served our purpose," Boxer said. "By that time we'll know too much . . . We already know too much, but he needs us—"

"He needs you," she corrected.

"That in his book is the same as needing us," Boxer told her, then squeezing her knee, he added, "Just don't panic . . . Keep calm."

"I'll try," she answered.

Boxer looked out of the window; they had left the coast, and were traveling inland—west, he guessed. And they were flying considerably lower, not more than a hundred feet off the ground, maybe less. To do that at night, the chopper pilot had to be very good.

Suddenly, Marcco sat up, and at the same time, the pilot announced over the PA system, "We're going in, boss."

The 'copter made a wide turn; its landing lights picked out a small clearing in, what looked like to Boxer, a wooded area. And just before they touched down, he glimpsed a white house, back of the tree line.

Boxer and Toni-Ann were hustled out of the chopper, and toward the white house. Before they reached it, the helicopter lifted off.

The house was farther away than it appeared to be, but there was a cleared path between it and the landing pad. Before they reached it, the door opened, and a man carrying a double-barreled shotgun stood in the doorway.

"Everything set, Vic?" Marcco called out.

"Sure," Vic answered. "Just have to wake the old man."

"That's your friend he's talking about," Marcco said to Boxer.

18

Vic disappeared into the house, and two lights came on. One in a front room, just off the door, and the other in a side room.

"From here, it's only a half-hour ride to the sub," Marcco said.

Boxer looked back at Vinny, who was following behind them. "Hey, Vinny, I forgot to tell you that if we get caught in three, maybe four hundred feet of water, you can escape through a hatch. All the submariners are trained to do that."

"Well, I ain't no fuckin' sub-whatcha call it," he answered.

"Yeah, but your old man is making sure you get the crash course," Boxer said.

Suddenly, Vinny shouted, "Fuck this!" And he bolted.

Boxer whirled around and ran after him.

"Stop the son-of-a-bitch!" Marcco screamed.

Vinny headed back toward the clearing.

Boxer was right behind him and gaining.

Marcco was screaming for a flashlight.

Boxer closed the distance between himself and Vinny, and made a flying tackle. Vinny went down, and before he could move, Boxer grabbed him in a headlock, pulled his gun out of its shoulder holster, and then cracked him over the head with it. Vinny went limp, and Boxer let go of him.

The two thugs were coming up fast; Marcco, Toni-Ann, and Vic were behind them.

The darkness was now changing into a pre-dawn grayness, and a mist was beginning to roll in.

Boxer hid in the trees.

"There's Vinny," one of the thugs yelled.

In a few moments, everyone was gathered around Vinny.

Boxer suddenly said, "Don't anyone move."

One of the thugs started to turn.

Boxer squeezed off a shot.

"Christ, I'm hit!" the man shouted, falling to the ground.

"All of you drop your guns," Boxer said.

"You're joking!" Marcco answered.

Boxer came up behind him, and put the muzzle of the .357 he'd taken from Vinny against the back of Marcco's head. "Now, do you still think I'm joking?"

His voice almost a squeak, Marcco said, "Do what he says."

The men dropped their guns.

"Get the guns, Toni-Ann . . . That's right; pick them up . . . Now bring me the shotgun," Boxer told her. He took the gun, made sure both barrels were loaded, slipped off the safety, and handing it back to Toni-Ann, he said, "We're going into the house—"

"Jack, is that you?"

"It's me, Admiral," Boxer called back. "Come on up here. I can use another hand."

"You did real good," Stark said, as soon as he saw what the situation was. "Real good."

"Take one of those guns, and we'll march these men back to the house," Boxer said.

Stark picked up another .357, and handing Boxer the remaining gun, a .38, he said, "Makes no sense to leave this kind of thing around." Then he looked at Vinny. "What shall we do about him?"

"He'll run for the woods, as soon as he comes to," Boxer said.

"Okay, gimpy," he said to the man he had wounded, "you just limp along . . . You'll be in a doctor's hands soon."

"But I'm bleeding—"

"We'll tie a tourniquet around it when we get to the house," Boxer said. "Now let's move."

The house was crudely furnished, with a table, three chairs, a wood-burning cooking stove, and an old icebox in the kitchen, and two beds in each of the other two rooms.

"There are two cars out back, and a pickup," Stark said.

"You'll never make it out of here alive," Marcco said morosely.

"If one of them moves, kill him," Boxer ordered.

Toni-Ann's eyes went wide.

"Stark, you take care of it," Boxer said.

"Wilco," the old man answered.

Boxer moved around the house, opening and shutting closet doors, then he went outside, and found a shed a few yards back into the trees. Inside, there were a dozen M-16s, five AK-47s, an assortment of small arms, and two grenade launchers, and ammunition for all of the weapons.

He helped himself to two M-16s, and fifty rounds for each, then he picked up the two grenade launchers, and a bag of grenades for them, and carried the weapons back to the house.

"All right, Marcco, now we pay your submarine a visit," Boxer announced.

"No way," Marcco said.

"And that's your final word?" Boxer asked.

Marcco nodded.

Boxer went into the kitchen, picked up a carving knife, and returning to the front room, he approached Marcco, and said, "Drop your pants, and your underwear."

"What?"

"I don't have time for games, Marcco," Boxer said. "You interrupted my vacation, kidnapped me and my friends—"

"Just what the fuck are you goin' to do?" Marcco questioned.

"I'm going to cut your balls off," Boxer calmly answered.

"You're crazy!"

"Maybe," Boxer said. "But just to show that I mean it, I'll slice a bit of your nose off."

Marcco's hand covered his face, and Boxer drew the blade across the man's knuckles.

Marcco screamed.

"Sooner or later, I'll get your balls," Boxer said, making another pass with the knife, this time cutting the back of Marcco's hand.

"I think I'm going to be sick," Toni-Ann said, and started to fall.

Boxer grabbed hold of her, and slapped her twice across the face.

With tears coming into her eyes, she managed to nod, and say, "I'm all right."

"Drop your pants and underwear, now!" Boxer suddenly roared.

"I'll take you to the boat," Marcco said. "I'll take you."

"Stark, tie Vic and the other two thugs up," Boxer said. "Put gags in their mouths, and put them in separate rooms . . . No, better still, tie them Indian fashion to separate trees."

"What about my leg?" the wounded man asked.

"It will be there by the time the doctor gets here," Boxer answered.

As soon as Stark was finished, Boxer designated Toni-Ann as the driver; Stark sat next to her, while he and Marcco occupied the rear seat.

"Okay, Marcco, give me the layout," Boxer said. "I want to know precisely where everything is before we get to the boat."

"The boat can't be seen . . . It's hidden under a shed. From the air it looks like any other fisherman's house . . . It's on an inlet that no one uses, about ten miles from the nearest town. At low tide, almost everything around it is mud flats, and at high tide, there's only enough water for the screw to work if the boat has no ballast at all."

"Go on," Boxer said.

"The roadway in is made of logs, and comes off the main road—it's really a dirt road, but it's higher by some four feet than the mud flats around it."

"And the log road, how high is that?" Boxer asked.

"Not very high. In spots, it's underwater at high tide."

"How long is the log roadway?" Boxer questioned.

"Maybe, a quarter of a mile."

"How many men?" Boxer asked.

"The crew, thirty—"

"I want the total number," Boxer demanded.

"Another five . . . Two cooks and three to guard the place," Marco answered.

Boxer rubbed his chin, which was already bristly . . . Even in a surprise attack, thirty-five men put the weight of firepower on the other side. . . .

"We'll stop in town," Boxer said. Then he asked, "What's its name?"

"Salt Creek, Georgia," Marcco answered.

"How far from Salt Creek to the sub?"

"Ten miles."

"What direction?"

Marcco shrugged. "Just keep going on the main road out until it becomes a dirt road, and you follow that until you reach the log road."

They reached Salt Creek in less than five minutes.

"The general store," Boxer said. "Park in front of it . . . Kill him if he tries to run, Stark."

"He'll stay put," Stark answered.

Boxer left the car. There was a chill in the morning air, and on the wind that came from the east, he could smell the salty tang of the ocean.

Boxer entered the store, and went straight up to the man behind the counter, who looked at him suspiciously.

"You have a public phone here?" Boxer asked.

"Over in the coffee shop," the man answered.

"Where's that?"

"Back a ways," the man said.

Boxer shook his head . . . He didn't have time to go back a ways . . . "You got a phone?" Boxer asked.

The man nodded.

"Where is it?"

The man hesitated.

"Listen, this is government business—"

"You don't look like no government man to me," the man said.

Boxer headed behind the counter to where the curtain was.

"You can't go in there!" the man protested.

Boxer shook his head, pulled back the curtain, went to the phone, and dialed the operator.

"That you, Luke?" the woman on the other end asked.

"No, it isn't Luke," Boxer said.

"Where's Luke?" she asked.

Boxer looked toward the man, and found himself looking at the business end of a shotgun. "Listen," he said, "you're going to have to use it, if you're going to try and stop me from making this call."

"Effy," Luke called out, "get the sheriff over here, quick."

"I've got to call Washington," Boxer said, speaking into the phone.

"You ain't callin' no one, 'till the sheriff says so," Effy answered.

Boxer suddenly felt as though he were in some sort of a sitcom, but this wasn't funny.

A white car with flashing red and blue lights screamed to a stop alongside Marcco's car. A tall man, wearing a straw cowboy hat, boots, and a .357 strode into the store. "Just what in the hell is goin' on here?" he asked in a booming voice.

"I'm trying to make a phone call," Boxer said . . . Here was a real life Smokey. . . .

"Okay, Luke, you tell me what's happening here?" the sheriff said.

"This man comes in, and asks if there was a public phone . . . I told him there was one in the coffee shop."

"I need to make that call, now," Boxer said.

"Who the hell are you?"

"Admiral Jack Boxer—"

"Sure you are," the storekeeper said. "Just like I'm a general."

"Let me make the call, and you can verify it," Boxer said, looking at the sheriff.

"What's so damn important about the call?" he asked.

"When I make it, you can listen to what I say," Boxer told him.

The sheriff's brow furrowed, and he took three steps toward the window. "Those your people out there?" he asked.

"Yes."

"They're not from around here."

"No . . . The one in the back and the woman are from New York."

"City people?"

"Let me make that call," Boxer said, "and I'll give you all the information you want."

"Effy, this is Sheriff Kirby . . . Put the call through for the man," the sheriff shouted.

"All right, now give me your name and the number you're callin'," Effy said.

Boxer gave his name, rank and the number for Pierce's home phone.

Pierce came on the line. "Where the hell are you?" he began. "Kahn—"

"Listen to me," Boxer said, "and listen very carefully . . ." And he quickly sketched the events that had happened, where he was, and what had to be done. "I need at least a fifty-man assault force here . . . Say within the hour."

"Marines from Camp Lejeune," Pierce said.

"Good."

"You want them to come by helos, or jump?"

"Better make it helos . . . That tide might be low when they arrive, and they'll wind up in the salt flats . . . Send in a couple of gunships . . . I want that sub shredded."

"You got it . . . Anything else?"

"Yeah, tell Kahn I have Marcco . . . Tell him, I'll be paying him a visit soon."

"Do you want the operation commander to be under your authority?" Pierce asked.

"What do you think?"

"It's up to you."

"I'll watch it from one of the gunships," Boxer said. "Have the pilot pick us up in front of the general store in Salt Creek."

"Can he land there?"

"Yes, in the roadway in front of the store," Boxer answered.

"A fine piece of work, though somewhat out of your area of operations," Pierce said.

"Somewhat," Boxer responded.

"Good luck," Pierce said.

Boxer thanked him and put the phone back in its cradle. Suddenly, he felt very tired.

"Was that for real?" Sheriff Kirby asked, pushing his straw hat up by its wide brim.

"It was for real," Boxer answered.

"You mean there's an enemy submarine out there on the flats?" Luke asked.

"Yes, you might call it an enemy submarine," Boxer said. "Maybe, it's more of an enemy than—" he was going to say the Russians, but remembered where he was, and didn't bother to finish what he'd started to say.

Boxer, Toni-Ann, and Stark—Marcco had been left with Sheriff Kirby, who would turn him over to the federal marshals— watched the operation from the open door of a chopper.

The Marines came in with ten troop carriers, and before the Marines landed, a lone chopper with a PA system positioned itself above the camouflaged sub, and demanded immediate surrender.

A couple of men showed themselves, and one pointed at the chopper. Then a third man came out, and made the mistake of firing an M-16 at the whirlybird.

About thirty seconds later the nine other helicopters came in from three sides, and the Marines deployed.

"All right," the man on the PA system said, "I want to see thirty-five men on the roadway, now."

The men on the sub trooped out to the roadway, and were immediately disarmed.

The operation was over, almost as soon as it had begun; then several Marines went into the shed to set explosive charges, and by the time the gunships began blasting away at the protective shed and the fuel storage area, there was nothing more to see, except the total destruction of the submarine, and that was something Boxer couldn't bring himself to watch.

"Let's head back to base," Boxer told the young pilot.

"Aye, aye, sir," the man answered.

19

Boxer and Toni-Ann escaped from the media people waiting for them at Camp Lejeune, and were flown back to New York in a Marine transport plane, while Stark was invited to spend a few days as a guest of the base commandant.

By the time Boxer and Toni-Ann were in a cab, on their way to Manhattan from Kennedy, where the transport had landed, it was after three in the afternoon.

Toni-Ann said, "At least a dozen people must be frantic to reach me, and Andrew must be out of his mind."

"I've been meaning to talk to you about him," Boxer said.

"To change the subject," Toni-Ann said, "would you have really cut his balls off?"

"Whose? Andrew's?"

"Don't be funny," she said. "I mean Marcco's . . . Would you have done it?"

Boxer noticed that the driver was looking at them in the rearview mirror, and Boxer bobbed his head toward the front of the cab.

"Now what?" Toni-Ann questioned.

Boxer dropped his voice to a whisper. "We're being tuned in."

"Oh!" Toni-Ann exclaimed.

"Now about Andrew," Boxer said. "I never wanted his balls."

Toni-Ann made a face, then she said, "Andrew is not up for discussion."

"What is?"

"Would you have done it?" she pressed.

"Done what?" Boxer asked, though he knew exactly what she was asking about."

"You can be a most infuriating man!"

"So I have been told . . . So I have been told," he responded with unmasked glee.

She made another moue and turned her face toward the window.

"But that's part of my charm," Boxer said.

Toni-Ann faced him. "For the last time, would you have cut his balls off?"

The cab suddenly veered violently to the left, throwing Boxer against the side and Toni-Ann against him. Then there was a screech of brakes and another jolt from behind that threw the two of them forward.

The cabbie turned onto the shoulder of the road and stopped. The other car came up behind them and also stopped.

"You folks okay?" the cabbie asked before he got out.

"I'm okay," Boxer said. "You okay?" he asked Toni-Ann.

"I'm okay," she answered.

"Good," the cabbie said, and went to meet the driver of the other vehicle, which, Boxer saw, was a green Lincoln Continental with a Connecticut plate.

"This is the way that other thing started," Boxer said.

"What other thing?" Toni-Ann asked.

Boxer shook his head and continued to look out of the back window. The driver of the Continental was a burly man with very red hair.

The two men appeared to be speaking amicably; they even shook hands, and the cabbie started back to the cab. The red-headed man got into his vehicle, revved the engine, and with squealing tires, he tried to squash the cabbie against the cab, before cutting into a line of traffic on the highway.

"Did you see that?" the cabbie asked, finally getting back into the cab.

"We saw it," Boxer answered. "Now, are you okay?"

"Yeah, the bastard never touched me," the cabbie answered, then he added, "There are a lot of nuts out there, and in this business you meet most of them."

Neither Boxer nor Toni-Ann had a response. But after a few moments of silence, Toni-Ann said, "You still haven't answered my question."

"All right, I'll answer it," Boxer said, paused, and asked, "What do you think I would have done?"

"That's not an answer."

"It's the best I can do," Boxer said.

Toni-Ann thought for a few moments. "From the look on your face then, I would say that you would have . . . But you could have been acting."

Boxer smiled. "That's something you'll never know, will you?"

"Any man who kills a shark—"

"That was something I had to do," Boxer said softly. "You were already safe in the boat when I went after the shark."

"I know that, and I could never understand why you did it," she said.

Boxer leaned back. "This isn't the time or the place to tell you about it," he said.

They were heading into the Brooklyn Battery Tunnel, and Boxer was aware that they didn't have too much more time together, unless she would go back to the Plaza with him. He turned to her. "Know what I'm thinking?"

"I think so," she answered in a throaty voice.

He took hold of her hand and brought the back of it to his lips. Then he said, "A few more hours won't make much of a difference to anyone."

"It might—to us."

"It will to me," Boxer said.

"To me too," Toni-Ann admitted.

Boxer put his arm around her, and drawing her to him, he said, "Maybe, if we spent some real time together, we could get a few things straightened out."

"Jack, in every way, you're an exciting, dynamic man, maybe too exciting at times, but—"

"Wait until you really get to know me!" he quipped.

"Let me finish," Toni-Ann said.

"Sounds as if you have been rehearsing."

"Maybe I have . . . Maybe I'm having trouble dealing with some of my feelings too."

"I'm not having any trouble dealing with mine," Boxer said.

"You're not making this easy for me," Toni-Ann complained.

"I want it to be so hard that you can't do it."

They were out of the tunnel, and moving along the West Side, which was already clogged with rush hour traffic, even though it was only four o'clock in the afternoon.

"The problem is—" Toni-Ann started to say.

"Is that you want my body," Boxer said, again aware of the fact that the driver was using the rearview mirror to look at him and Toni-Ann.

"Be serious!"

"I am, and I want your body," Boxer said.

She was quiet for several moments, then she told him that she didn't really know him.

"You're absolutely right. But what you seem to be ignoring is that I'm offering you the chance to change that," Boxer said. "We sure as hell are not going to get to know one another if we don't take the opportunity—every opportunity—to spend time together."

"What you don't realize is that I'm engaged, that in less than a month, three weeks to the day, I will be married."

"Ah, as the expression goes, 'What goes around comes around,'" Boxer commented.

"Now what the hell is that supposed to mean?"

"Andrew—we've come back to him."

"No way . . . I'm not going to let myself get trapped into a discussion about him."

"Not about him, about you," Boxer said, as they passed the Intrepid Air Museum.

"What about me?"

"You're letting something go by that you may never have again," Boxer said.

"You?"

"Me . . . Love . . . Passion."

"What about just plain old security, reliability . . . things like that?"

Boxer wasn't about to tell her that he was a millionaire several times over, and that in terms of financial security he would be able to give everything that Andrew could and probably more. He wanted her decision to go with him, if she made it, to be based on her need for him, not on how much money he had.

"You haven't answered me," she chided.

"After what you have seen, I must have some reliability in your eyes," he said. "After all, you're here, and alive . . . Doesn't that give me some Brownie points?"

"You're beginning to make me sound mercenary, and I'm really not," Toni-Ann said.

Boxer shrugged.

"All right, what about the difference between our ages . . . You're more than twenty years older than I am."

"So that's in the kettle too," Boxer scoffed. "A mere twenty years between us . . . That only proves two things: the first is that I have excellent taste, at least as far as choosing a woman goes, and secondly, you have excellent taste for allowing yourself to be chosen by someone like myself . . . After all, I'm not your everyday kind of a shark killer, now am I?" Even as he spoke, Boxer realized they'd turned up Fifty-Seventh Street, and it would be a matter of five minutes at the very most before they were at the Plaza.

"You want me to give everything up for—"

"No, I want you to have what you really want," Boxer said.

"Never in my wildest imaginings had I ever pictured myself as—"

Boxer put his finger gently across her lips. "Don't say the wrong word," he told her.

"Then tell me the right word," Toni-Ann responded.

"First come with me," he said.

The cab rolled to a stop in front of the hotel.

"You have a decision to make, now," Boxer told her.

As the hotel doorman opened the cab door, she gave Boxer her hand, and whispered, "I'll go with you, at least for now."

Boxer smiled, and said, "Now, that's what I call a reasonable decision."

Moments later they were out of the cab and greeted by a dozen newspaper people, including several on-the-spot TV reporters.

"This isn't exactly what I thought was going to happen," Toni-Ann said.

"Neither did I," Boxer answered. "But there's no way to avoid it, and besides, it's as good a time as any to announce our forthcoming marriage."

"Don't joke—"

"It's not a *joke*. I'm serious. I want to marry you."

"You don't even know me."

"Knowing you will come later . . . It will add an element of discovery to our marriage . . . I will discover you, and you will discover me . . . Will you marry me?"

"I don't see how I could refuse, especially with all these reporters and TV people present."

"All right, let's go tell the world, or at the very least all of those people who watch the six o'clock news that we are going to be married," Boxer said, and with Toni-Ann in tow, he headed straight for the TV cameras that were set up in the hotel's lobby.

Boxer finished the TV interview by saying, "The war against drugs is a real war. If the enemy uses a submarine to wage it, then we have no choice but to use the necessary countermeasures to insure the safety of our people."

"Does that mean you advocate the use of the armed forces to fight the drug war?" one of the TV people asked him.

"I don't think my statement can be misinterpreted," Boxer answered, taking hold of Toni-Ann's forearm. Then he said, "Now, if you will excuse us, and"— he flashed a broad smile— "and even if you won't, we have several very important things to do." He quickly managed to steer Toni-Ann toward one of the elevator banks, then into a car, and within a matter of seconds, the door closed, and they were on their way up.

As soon as Boxer opened the door to the room and switched on the light, the phone began to ring, and he saw several large floral arrangements and a wine cooler with two magnums of champagne.

"I'll answer the phone," Boxer said. "You check out who's responsible for the—" he hesitated, then said, "goodies."

Toni-Ann laughed. "Hard to say that, wasn't it?"

"Like swallowing a frog," he answered truthfully.

"Phone is still ringing," Toni-Ann said, pointing to it.

Boxer picked it up, and before he could speak, the voice on the other end said, "This is Igor."

"Igor!" Boxer exclaimed, and shouted to Toni-Ann, "It's Igor . . . Where the hell are you?"

"Washington . . . I decided to come a few days earlier to show Galena the sights . . . Nowadays we can do things like that."

"Wonderful, absolutely wonderful . . . Listen, suppose you and Galena come here, or if it would be easier for you, Toni-Ann and I will come down there . . . I know Stark wants to see you . . . We could go out to the house. There's room enough for all of us."

Borodine emitted a long whistle. "You're going at flank speed, Admiral," Borodine laughed. "You have to come back to Washington anyway, so why don't you bring Toni-Ann—"

"Sure I will—"

"Let me finish," Borodine said.

"I'm listening."

"You bring her down here, then the four of us will go out to the house, and spend a long weekend there. I don't have to be at my desk officially until next Wednesday."

"That's great, really great!" Boxer exclaimed.

"You can reach me at the Carlton," Borodine said, with obvious pride.

"You must be coming up in the world," Boxer responded.

"I'm almost a diplomat now," Borodine said.

"And I'm still the same—you know, I really don't know what the hell I am," Boxer admitted, his tone suddenly changed. He had thought about that before Marcco had entered his life . . . Maybe, he realized, that was why he wanted to go back to the places he had known as a boy. Maybe, he was looking for himself?

"You're the best damn submarine skipper in the world," Borodine said.

"I won't argue that," Boxer said, quickly slipping back into his former mood.

"At least have the courtesy to—"

"All right, we're the best."

"That's more like it," Borodine laughed. "Now tell me when you're coming to Washington."

"Today is Tuesday . . . I'll be down by Friday morning, and we'll drive out to the house before lunch."

"Wonderful, Jack . . . See you soon," Borodine said.

"See you," Boxer answered, and replaced the phone in its cradle. "That was Admiral Igor Borodine, my Russian friend."

"I gathered that much from the phone conversation," she said.

"Who sent the flowers and the champagne?" Boxer answered.

"The hotel is responsible for the champagne, one of the floral displays came from Stark, another from your EXO, whatever that means—"

"My executive officer," Boxer explained.

"Oh!"

"And the third floral display?"

"Admiral Pierce," she said.

"He's the CNO, Chief of Naval Operations . . . the boss man in the navy," . . . Boxer said.

Toni-Ann accepted the explanation with a nod, then said, "I've got to shower . . . Suddenly, I feel yukky."

"I can't say that I feel much different," Boxer said. "Do you suppose it would be possible for us to share the same shower?"

Before Toni-Ann could answer, the phone rang again.

Boxer picked it up, and said, "Boxer here."

"This is Kahn," the voice on the other end said.

"You're the last person I want to talk to," Boxer told him.

"I want you here in my office tomorrow morning," Kahn said.

Boxer glanced at Toni-Ann, then in a hard, but calm voice, he said, "That's out of the question."

"That's—"

"Don't tell me that's an order," Boxer growled.

"Another lady is down," Kahn said.

"Holy Christ!" Boxer exclaimed. "Which one?"

"We're not on a secure line," Kahn reminded him.

"Yeah, I know . . . I'll be there about two."

"Ten o'clock in the morning."

"I said two," Boxer barked, and slammed the phone down. Right at that moment he couldn't think of anyone he disliked more than Kahn.

"What was all that about?" Toni-Ann questioned, moving close to him.

"The head of the Company," Boxer said.

"You mean the Company, the CIA?" Toni-Ann asked.

Boxer nodded. "He was one of the men who came down to see me when I was at the Hawksbill."

Toni-Ann gave him a peculiar look. "What's your connection to them?"

Boxer shook his head.

"You won't, or can't, tell me?" she asked.

"Both." Then he said, "I have to be back in Washington tomorrow afternoon . . . There's an emergency."

Toni-Ann looked at him, and said, "This is the way it's going to be, isn't it?"

Boxer immediately understood what she meant, and taking her into his arms, he answered, "No . . . But you will just have to trust me on that . . . I can't give you any guarantees."

She rested against him for several moments, then she said, "Let's take the shower."

"Good idea," Boxer said. "But before I do, I'm going to call the switchboard and tell them to hold all calls."

Toni-Ann nodded approvingly, and beckoning to him with her finger, she led him into the bathroom.

"You're beautiful," Boxer said, looking at Toni-Ann, stretched out naked on the bed.

"You only say that when I don't have any clothes on," she told him, extending her arms up to him.

He eased himself down into her embrace. "I guess it's easier to appreciate you when you don't have anything on," he said, enjoying the softness of her breasts against his chest, and kissing the tip of her nose, then her lips.

"You do know I love you," she said in a low voice.

"Yes, I know it," he answered, moving his lips to the turgid nipple of her right breast, then to the left, then down to the hollow of her stomach, and finally to the already wet vaginal lips.

Even as she sighed, a slight tremor shook Toni-Ann's body. "That feels so wonderful!"

Boxer used his tongue on her clit, making her writhe with pleasure and moan with delight.

"You keep doing that just that way, and you're going

to send me into orbit," she told him, caressing the top of his head.

"Is that where you want to be?"

"Now, I want to be wherever you want me," she answered.

"Do me," he said, moving around to enable her to reach his penis.

Within moments, Toni-Ann had his phallus in her mouth, and his whole being reacted to the heat of her lips, the delicate movements of her tongue on the head of his penis, and just below it, on the shaft.

Boxer kissed the insides of her naked thighs, then went back to her clit. He relished the taste and musky scent of her.

She moved her lips down to his scrotum, sending hot tendrils of incredible pleasure rocketing through his body, and clouding out his thoughts with a delicious smokiness. . . .

Boxer ran his hands over her breasts, down under her buttock, and even as he continued to mouth her sex, he gently eased his finger into her anus.

"Oh my God!" Toni-Ann exclaimed. "Oh my God!" And placing her open mouth against one of his balls, she made a slight humming sound.

The vibration fueled his passion even more. The fire in his groin now raged.

"Jack, come inside of me," Toni-Ann called out in a breathless voice. "Come inside of me!"

Boxer quickly positioned her above him, purposefully giving her the added pleasure of dominance, while he took delight in being able to either reach behind her, to her buttock or under her, to her vagina.

She moved low over him, and asked him to suck on her nipples.

"You mean like this?" he asked, drawing the nipple of her left breast between his lips and sucking hard on it.

"Oh yes, yes . . . Do the other one, now!"

Boxer moved his lips to the right nipple, and at the same time, he caressed her clit.

She began to slide up and down his penal shaft, slowly at first, then with increasing rapidity.

Boxer met her movements with thrusts that kept pace with her motion.

She bent her face down to his, pressing her lips on his, and at the same time, not only moved up and down, but also rolled her hips.

The combination of movements made Boxer thrust even harder and deeper into her.

Toni-Ann began to moan and dig her fingernails into Boxer's back.

He could feel the tension make her body coil tighter and tighter . . . And the tighter it became, the faster she moved.

He was moments away from his own orgasmic explosion, when suddenly Toni-Ann screamed, "Fuck me . . . Fuck me . . . I'm there . . . I'm there!" And she raked his back with her nails.

Boxer's cum gushed out of him, and bringing her down, he buried his face in the moist, warm valley between her breasts, while the explosion of pleasure rose up from his groin, flooding his brain, anesthetizing it with the smoke of spent passion. . . .

For minutes neither of them spoke, then gently they separated, and Toni-Ann said, "I'm tired . . . I'd like to sleep, now." She nestled against him, her bare breasts on his chest, and one naked thigh over his, so that the top of his thigh rested against her love mound.

Boxer closed his eyes and quickly fell into a deep sleep. And then he was just as quickly awake.

Toni-Ann was no longer next to him.

Boxer slipped his hand behind his head. He didn't bother to call her name. He knew she'd left him. He knew she would the moment she had asked him how he was connected to the Company. He took a deep breath, and slowly exhaling, uttered a ragged sigh. . . .

20

At precisely two o'clock, Boxer was in Kahn's office, a large room with two windows, and furnished with an ornate, Louis XIV desk, several French Provincial chairs and small tables, and several very large landscape paintings on the walls.

Boxer was somewhat surprised that he was the only one there. He had, at least, expected Pierce to have been invited. But this was obviously Kahn's show.

Boxer sat across from Kahn, waiting to be told about the boat that was down. But Kahn was more interested in riffling through some papers than in talking to him.

Boxer filled his pipe and lit it. Then after blowing a column of smoke up toward the ceiling, his voice exploded. "You have three fucking minutes, Kahn, to stop playing your head game and tell me about the boat, or I walk."

Kahn's head jerked up.

Boxer looked at his watch. "Starting now!"

"You wouldn't dare—"

"Listen, Kahn, you should know me well enough by

now to know that you couldn't begin to imagine what I would or would not dare."

Kahn put down the papers he'd been holding. "You ruined one of my operations," he said acidly. "Single-handed you destroyed an operation that has taken me two years to put together."

Boxer took the pipe out of his mouth, pointed it at Kahn, and said, "Marcco works for you?"

"In a manner of speaking—"

Boxer was off the chair. "Just what the fuck does 'a manner of speaking' mean, Kahn? Either he does or doesn't."

"Marcco and the Company had an arrangement," Kahn said.

Boxer was becoming more and more angry. "Did that sweet arrangement you had with the slime ball happen to include kidnapping me, Toni-Ann, and Stark?"

"Ah yes, I forgot to congratulate you on your forthcoming wedding . . . Congratulations."

Enraged now, Boxer leaned across the desk and shouted in Kahn's face, "Give me a fucking answer, now!"

Kahn shrank back. "I'd advise you to—"

Boxer shot out his hand, grabbed hold of Kahn by his necktie, and wrenched the man toward him. "Your arrangement almost got three people killed," he barked.

"It wasn't supposed to happen the way it did," Kahn squeaked.

Boxer let go of the man's necktie. "Tell me how it was supposed to happen."

Kahn straightened up and rubbed the back of his neck.

"See your chiropractor later," Boxer said. "Your neck

is going to hurt for awhile."

"Thanks a lot!" Kahn answered sarcastically. "I'll send you the bill."

"Stop whining . . . Just tell me what was supposed to happen," Boxer said, sitting down again.

"You weren't supposed to be involved at all," Kahn answered, loosening his tie and unbuttoning the collar button of his shirt.

"Marcco used the boat to transport drugs."

"I don't need you to tell me that."

"We made it possible for him to get the boat, and we put a crew together for him," Kahn said.

"So the stories about the Company being in the drug business aren't just stories after all?"

Kahn ignored the question. "The former captain—well, he met with an unfortunate accident."

"By unfortunate, you mean Marcco, or one of his men, killed him because he became greedy."

"Something like that. But how did you know—"

"Marcco told me," Boxer said.

"Your involvement with Marcco's son—"

"Now there's a remarkable specimen of human garbage, if there ever was one," Boxer commented.

Rubbing the back of his neck, Kahn said, "Two coincidences set things up. The first took place at the Hawksbill, when Marcco found out who you were; then when you had his son arrested—well, he needed someone to skipper his submarine, and you just happened to be there."

"All right, there's some kind of a logic behind what you just told me; now, tell me the rest of it."

"There isn't any 'rest of it' to tell," Kahn said.

Boxer put his hand out and rapidly moved his fingers toward himself. "Give," he said. "I want to know about the entire operation."

"You already know more than you should," Kahn answered.

"I want the rest of it," Boxer said, "or I go on national TV tonight, and tell them exactly what you told me."

Kahn blanched.

"I'm listening," Boxer said, "and I don't hear anything, yet."

"It's complicated . . . There are political reasons why it was done," Kahn said. "Marcco has certain connections whom we wanted on our side. They would remain on our side, just as long as we did not interfere with their business."

"Marcco was the middle man?"

"Something like that," Kahn answered.

Boxer slapped his thigh, stood up, and said, "So you get what you want, Marcco gets what he wants, and the fucking druggies get what they want . . . Everyone is happy!" He shook his head. "The whole thing makes me want to puke."

Kahn didn't answer.

Again Boxer shook his head. Between Toni-Ann walking out on him and what he'd just learned, he was angry and frustrated.

"There's the other problem, and we still have to deal with it," he said.

Boxer nodded. "What boat is down?"

"None," Kahn said.

Boxer could feel the color come into his cheeks.

"I knew that the only way I could get you here was to

tell you that a boat was down," Kahn admitted.

Boxer wanted to grab hold of him again, and this time, really hurt him . . . If he hadn't called, Toni-Ann wouldn't have gone. She— Boxer restrained himself. He took several deep breaths, and told himself that, sooner or later, she would have found out that he worked for the Company, and she would have left him. . . .

"By a week from this coming Monday, you'll take command of the attack submarine *Scorpion* . . . She's in Norfolk now being fitted for a special mission."

"What mission?" Boxer asked suspiciously.

"A bogus scientific one," Kahn answered. "There will be two men on board posing as scientists, but they are Office of Naval Intelligence agents."

"Why that boat in particular?"

"She's had a series of problems that ranged from an unexplained fire in the forward torpedo room to alarms either failing to go off when they should, or going off when they shouldn't."

Boxer nodded.

"You're going to do deep dives," Kahn said.

"Where?"

"Not too far away . . . The Baltimore Canyon."

Again Boxer nodded . . . The canyon was over five thousand feet deep.

"You'll be out for two days, back for two . . . That will give some authenticity to the idea of having scientists on board."

"Will I actually skipper the boat?" Boxer questioned.

"Yes . . . Originally, you were to go aboard as a replacement officer, but now that you've been on national TV, there's no way for you to pretend to be someone else."

Boxer leaned forward and rested his elbows on the desk. "I need to know everything you know about that boat, and what has happened on it . . . If you play games with me this time, Kahn, your neck won't hurt . . . You won't be able to feel a thing . . . You'll be dead. Do you understand exactly what I am telling you?"

Kahn nodded.

"I want to hear it," Boxer told him in a cold, hard voice.

"I understand," Kahn said, then reaching into the middle drawer of his desk, he took out a sealed envelope. "There's a report on every incident here . . . This is a duplicate file. After you read it, destroy it."

"It will be destroyed," Boxer assured him.

"Just so that you know where you stand with me," Kahn said, "everything that has happened here this afternoon has been videotaped."

"With sound, no doubt," Boxer said, as he stood up to go.

"Just something to use against you should the necessity ever arise," Kahn said.

Boxer didn't answer.

"I don't imagine we have anything else to say to each other?" Kahn said.

"Nothing," Boxer answered, and picking up the sealed envelope, he turned and left Kahn's office.

Boxer returned to New York that evening. He had thought about going down to spend time with Stark, but he realized that he would be less than agreeable company.

He decided to spend another couple of days in the city doing what he'd originally started out to do.

The cab ride back to the city from LaGuardia took less time than he thought it would, and he arrived at the Plaza by seven o'clock at night.

He stopped at the front desk, and asked the clerk if there were any messages for him.

"These came," the clerk said, handing him a large stack of telegrams. "And many more floral pieces and several baskets of fruit . . . All of them were put in your suite . . . The management has also instructed me to tell you that there is no charge for your stay here, or for anything you might order from our various restaurants or the bar."

"Thank you," Boxer said. "I would like to donate the various baskets of fruit to the children's section of Bellview Hospital, as well as the flowers."

"I'll see that it is taken care of, Admiral," the desk clerk answered.

Boxer almost expected the man to salute. Had he, Boxer knew he would have returned it. Instead, he smiled and thanked him, then he headed for the elevators.

He shared the car with a young couple who were obviously either newlyweds or lovers there for a night. The young man was in his late twenties or early thirties. The woman, somewhere around Toni-Ann's age. The young man had his arm around her waist, and she was leaning against him. They were oblivious to the fact that someone else was in the car with them, and Boxer was envious of the young man. . . .

The car stopped, and the couple left it.

Alone now, Boxer was faced with the reality of how he

was going to spend the rest of the evening. By the time the elevator stopped at his floor and he walked out of the open door, he decided that he would go down to Chinatown for dinner. He knew several restaurants there, and even some people, because of a previous assignment that involved Chinese people.

Boxer reached the door of his suite, unlocked it, and when he stepped inside, he saw that the lights in both rooms were on. Alert, he moved cautiously . . . Someone from the hotel might have left the lights on, or it could be one of Marcco's—

"Jack?"

Boxer stopped short, his heart skipped a beat, and then raced. He swallowed hard, and managed to call out, "Toni-Ann?"

Wearing a diaphanous teal blue negligee, she stood framed by the doorway between the sitting room and the bedroom.

"I thought you—" Boxer started to say.

"I had," she told him.

He moved closer to her. "Why the change?"

"Because . . ." she started toward him. "Because, you are exciting, dynamic, and—"

He took her into his arms. "And what?"

"And I like the way you love me, touch me, do all of the things you do," she told him, offering her lips to him.

Boxer kissed her hungrily: her lips, her neck, her eyelids, the bare tops of her breasts, and the valley between them. "I love you," he said. "I love you."

"I love you," she answered. "I love you, Jack Boxer."

He swept her up into his arms and carried her into the bedroom.

"Make love to me," she said.

"I'm not going to 'make' anything," Boxer said, gently putting her down on the bed. "But I am going to love you."

Toni-Ann nodded, sat up and stripping off the negligee, she said, "It would only get in the way."

Boxer laughed, stripped, and settled alongside her.

"No, come on top of me," Toni-Ann said. "Ah, yes . . . That feels good, Jack . . . It feels so very good."

Boxer kissed her closed eyelids, and began to move, knowing he would ride her and himself to ecstasy. . . .

21

Boxer and Toni-Ann sat in a rented Chevy Caprice at the foot of the quay where the *Scorpion* was moored. Boxer had already brought his gear aboard the previous day, when the only officer aboard was JG Thomas Freel, who had almost gone into cardiac arrest when Boxer reported to him.

Toni-Ann nestled against Boxer. "I've said goodbye to many people, many, many times. But this is the hardest—"

"I'll be back in seventy-two hours, and you'll be right here to meet me," Boxer said to reassure her. "This is just a routine dive." He hadn't told her anything about the mission.

"I'll be here," she answered, offering her lips for him to kiss.

"When I'm back, we'll make the necessary arrangements for the wedding . . . I don't see the need for a large reception."

"Neither do I," Toni-Ann agreed.

"I'd like to have it in Washington, if that's all right

with you?" Boxer said.

"No reason why my friends couldn't come down—"

"I'll take care of their hotel arrangements," Boxer offered.

She squeezed his arm. "That's sweet . . . but unnecessary." Then she said, "I really liked Galena and Igor."

"They liked you too," Boxer answered.

"Galena said that you saved Igor's life—"

"He saved mine a few times too."

"A few times?"

Boxer smiled. "It's kind of hard to understand . . . sometimes I don't even understand how it happened that the two of us became friends. But we did."

"After seeing the two of you together, I can't imagine you being anything else."

"I'll admit that it's not easy, especially now," Boxer answered. "But there was a time when we tried to kill each other . . . not out of hate, but because that's what our governments ordered us to do."

Toni-Ann trembled, and in a whisper she said, "Thank God neither of you succeeded."

Momentarily, Boxer clasped her tightly to him . . . Boxer had never thought about God having a role in his relationship with Borodine. For him, and he knew for Borodine as well, there was a mutual respect that was there from their very first encounter; each of them recognized it, and was aware of its uniqueness.

"Too bad you can't call me on the telephone," Toni-Ann said. "I'd feel a lot better about not having you here."

"We'll use mental telepathy," Boxer said, running his hand over her thigh, then he added, "I love you."

Toni-Ann pressed herself closer to him.

"If there's anything you need, give Stark a call," Boxer told her.

She nodded. "I'm going up to New York. I have several things at the magazine that have to be done. I'll be back here in time to meet you."

Another car pulled into the parking area. A woman was at the wheel, and an officer sat next to her. They kissed, passionately, then the officer left the car, and started the long walk to the end of the quay, where the *Scorpion* was tied up.

"It's time for me to go," Boxer said. "I have to meet my staff."

"Will you sail immediately?" she asked.

"Yes, we'll get under way as soon as the full crew is aboard," Boxer said. Then with a slight smile, he added, "My guess is that everyone is aboard."

She looked at him questioningly.

"That JG probably passed the word that the new skipper is flag rank," Boxer said.

"Is that unusual—I mean, for an admiral to be the skipper of a submarine, or for that matter any boat?"

"Ship," he corrected, then said, "Very unusual . . . An admiral's job is—"

"What's wrong?"

He shook his head. "This isn't the time or the place for you to learn something about the navy chain of command . . . The only thing I will tell is that I am—as far as I know—the only admiral who also has direct command of vessels of any type."

"I told you, you were unique," she said.

"I must go," Boxer said.

This time she turned fully to him.

Boxer kissed her passionately, moving his tongue against hers.

She took hold of his hand and put it over her breast.

"Take care of yourself," Boxer said, finally opening the door and drawing away from her.

"You too," she responded.

Boxer left the car, closed the door, blew her a kiss, and turning toward the pier, he began the long walk to the boat. Once he looked back and waved.

She waved back.

The farther out on the pier he got, the more he felt the cold, blustery, northeast wind, and more aware he became of the chop it caused in the bay. He glanced up at the sky. It was covered with gray clouds.

Boxer reached the *Scorpion*, and before he stepped aboard, he saluted the flag on the aft jack staff, then reported to the duty officer, Lieutenant Chester, according to his name tag.

"Full crew aboard?" Boxer asked.

"Yes, sir," Chester answered.

"Does that include our two guests: Misters Howell and Rampel?"

"Yes, sir, they've been aboard since thirteen hundred," Chester responded.

"Pass the word I'm on board, and have the crew stand by to get under way," Boxer said.

"Aye, aye, sir," Chester said, saluting.

Boxer returned the salute, then as he started to climb the ladder on the side of sail to the outside bridge, the MC5 came on. "All hands, now hear this . . . All hands, now hear this, the captain is aboard . . . All hands, the captain is aboard . . ." There was a momentary pause before the same voice called, "All hands, now hear this, stand by to get under way . . . All hands, stand by to get under way."

Within moments, the bridge detail scrambled up through the open hatchway directly behind Boxer. Two lookouts covered the port and starboard sides.

The EXO, Steven Phillips, saluted Boxer, and said, "Welcome aboard, sir."

Boxer returned the salute, and answered with the customary, "Glad to be aboard."

The fore and aft deck details were ready at the lines that secured the boat to the pier.

"Take her out, Captain," Boxer said to Phillips. By using the man's rank rather than his name, he was putting him on notice that he would be judging his skill, and that he wanted to keep a very definite line between himself and the crew, which was contrary to the usual blurring of rank aboard submarines. But he did not want to form a relationship with any member of the crew that might in some way influence his judgment, or his ability to deal with a problem.

After a momentary pause, Phillips answered, "Aye, aye, sir." And stepping slightly forward to the control console, he switched on the PA system and ordered the fore line and then the aft lines to be cast off.

The combination of wind and tide moved the boat away from the pier.

Phillips called for 'slow ahead' from the engine room by dialing the speed on the control console.

"Ease the helm over to the port," he ordered.

"Easing the helm over to the port," the bridge

helmsman answered.

The *Scorpion* began to angle away from the concrete pier, creating a ribbon of white wake.

"Normal helm," Phillips said.

"Normal helm," the helmsman answered.

"Steady as she goes," Phillips ordered.

The helmsman repeated the order.

Boxer looked back toward the land. Toni-Ann was standing in front of the car. He waved, hoping she could see him.

She waved back.

"Freighter, three points off the starb'd bow," the starboard lookout called.

Phillips nodded, then he said, "Come to new course three five degrees."

"Coming to course three five degrees," the helmsman answered.

The boat was now turning parallel to the western shore of the Chesapeake.

"One-third ahead," Phillips said, dialing in the change of speed to the engine room from the control console.

The boat's movement quickened, and her wake became a white furrow in the bay's gray water.

They slid past the various piers where the carriers *Midway*, *Oriskiny*, and *Kennedy* were tied up, then they passed the freighter, the *Kobe Maru*, a huge container-carrying vessel.

The bay widened, and off in the distance, directly in front of them, was the dark gray outline of the Chesapeake Bay Bridge and Tunnel complex that connected the eastern and western shores of the bay at its mouth.

"We'll dive as soon as we clear a hundred feet of water on the other side of the bridge," Boxer said.

"Aye, aye, sir," Phillips answered.

Boxer checked the fathometer. There was more than a hundred and twenty-five feet below them.

A wind-driven rain began to fall, obscuring the bridge, and everything else that wasn't within a dozen yards of the boat.

Boxer pulled the hood of his sea coat over his head.

"All engines, slow ahead," Phillips called, once again dialing in a change of speed. Then he called down to the radar officer, "Report all targets within five hundred yards." A moment passed, then he said, "Scope clear."

Several minutes passed, and no one on the bridge said anything. Then suddenly the red signal light from communications began to flash.

Phillips opened the line, putting it on the speaker.

"Sir, we have a May Day from an Atlantic Airways plane," the communications officer said, struggling to keep his voice normal.

"Position?"

The COMMO gave the latitude and longitude.

Phillips dialed the two coordinates into the navigation computer, and within a fraction of a second, the boat's position with relation to the aircraft's was displayed as a red line between two red circles, and the time it would take the boat to cover the distance between the two circles, traveling at flank speed on the surface or underwater.

"I have the Conn," Boxer said, taking command, then he said, "Radio, we are responding . . . Send the same message to NORLANT SUBCOM."

"Aye, aye, sir," the COMMO answered.

"Captain, you coordinate the various aspects of the mission," Boxer said. "We'll dive, as soon as we can . . . That means we'll be down about sixty feet, once we clear the bridge . . . Check the charts for the depth in the area where the plane expects to crash land."

"Aye, aye, sir," Phillips answered.

"Alert our divers . . . They'll have their work cut out for them," Boxer said. "Canvass the crew for additional volunteer divers . . . We'll need them."

"Aye, aye, sir," Phillips answered, and dropped down through the hatchway.

Boxer signaled the COMMO. "Is the plane still airborne?"

"It is circling the area . . . Two engines are out."

"Roger that," Boxer answered, and peered into the lashing rain to catch sight of the Bay Bridge.

The *Scorpion* was down two hundred and fifty feet and moving at fifty knots.

Boxer was in the control room. All systems were go.

Phillips was at the boat's master control computer. "We should be at the crash site within nine minutes," he said.

"The plane has already been down for six," Boxer said.

"We're just below reactor-red," Phillips answered.

Boxer pursed his lips . . . Reactor-red meant that they were operating very near the danger point . . . but as a safety precaution that exact value was always displayed before the reactor's operating conditions came anywhere near it.

"In the red zone," Phillips answered.

Boxer checked the boat's speed; it was up to fifty-five knots. "Maintain present speed," he said.

"Aye, aye, sir," Phillips answered.

"Target, bearing, two five degrees . . . Range, thirty thousand yards . . . Dead in the water."

"That must be the plane," Boxer said. He checked the sonar display. "Captain, notify base that we have located the aircraft."

"Aye, aye, sir," Phillips responded.

"Stand by to surface," Boxer said, and touched the Klaxon button three times. Then to the DO he said, "Get us topside as quickly as possible."

"Aye, aye, sir," the DO answered.

The planesman eased back, bringing the planes to ten degrees.

The boat's bow rose.

"Blowing all tanks," the DO said.

The *Scorpion* surged up toward the surface.

"Ease off at fifty feet," Boxer said, watching the overhead depth gauge unwind. "Then take up."

"Aye, aye, sir," the DO answered.

Boxer's eyes automatically went to the fathometer: the bottom was eight hundred feet down.

"Coming to fifty feet," the DO announced. "Leveling—"

A sudden explosion shook the *Scorpion.*

Instantly, the automatic emergency Klaxon started to scream.

Boxer shut it down. His eyes went to the depth gauge. They were going down. "Blow all ballast!" he ordered.

"Blowing all ballast," the DO answered.

The fire alarm started to wail.

"All ballast blown," the DO reported.

Boxer checked the depth gauge. They were passing through the three hundred foot level and still going down. He signaled the COMMO. "Send a May Day . . . Give our exact position. Indicate that we have had an explosion on board, and we are on fire," he said in a clear, steady voice.

"Aye, aye, sir," the COMMO said.

22

Boxer switched on the 5MC. "All hands, now hear this . . . All hands, now hear this . . . This is Admiral Boxer . . . We are operating on one scrubber . . . That means that after thirty hours the scrubber won't be able to produce clean air, and that means that all unnecessary activity will be curtailed. Every man will remain at his duty station, but no activity will take place. I have been informed by the CNO that a coördinated rescue operation is on the way." He switched off the 5MC, moved to the side of the control room, found a place near a bulkhead wall, and sat down on the deck.

The other officers and enlisted men followed Boxer's example, and chose places where they would be as comfortable as possible.

Boxer closed his eyes . . . There was certainly an irony in having a major accident while on the way to rescue victims of another disaster. By now, the whole world knew that the *Scorpion* was down . . . Boxer momentarily bit his lower lip . . . Stark, whatever his fears, would be able to handle it. But he wasn't all that sure about Toni-Ann. . . .

"Sir, engineering is signaling," one of the junior officers said.

Boxer scrambled to his feet, went to the control console, and connected the control room to engineering. "Boxer here," he said.

"Sir, the ambient temperature has fallen two degrees, and is continuing to fall," the engineering officer reported.

"What is the water temp?" Boxer questioned.

"Forty degrees, sir," the man answered.

Boxer took a deep breath, and as he slowly exhaled, he checked the temperature gauge. It was sixty-eight degrees. By the time it reached forty, the inside of the boat would feel like the inside of a refrigerator. "Have you any indication why this is happening?"

"The thermostats are tied into the air system . . . They cycle in relation to the ambient temp of the boat's air."

"Did you try to override the main connections?" Boxer questioned.

"Yes, sir. But it couldn't be done."

"Keep trying," Boxer told him.

"Aye, aye, sir," the EO answered.

Boxer switched off the 5MC, moved over to Phillips, and squatting down next to him, explained the latest development. Then he said, "Have the men, in small groups, get hold of warm clothing before the quality of the air begins to change."

"Yes, sir," Phillips answered, beginning to stand.

Boxer went to the two ONI agents. "We're going to be a lot colder down here before too much more time passes . . . Better get the warmest clothes you have."

Both men nodded, then the older-looking of the two, whose name tag read Martins, calmly asked, "Do you have any lethal pills—cyanide-type—aboard?"

Boxer raised his eyebrows.

"If it should come down to it—well, I'd rather check out that way, than by suffocation."

"No one is going to *check out*, as you put it," Boxer answered angrily. "No one!" Aware that the other men in the control room were now staring at him, he said, "Everyone, listen up . . . If we stay calm, every one of us will get out alive, and with luck, we'll be able to bring the *Scorpion* to the surface, and sail her into Norfolk."

Some of the men nodded, and smiled at him, but a few had doubt in their eyes, and one or two couldn't look at him.

Boxer returned to where he had been, sat down, and closing his eyes, he leaned against the bulkhead wall. He thought about Toni-Ann, their lovemaking, how she looked in the nude, even the way her sex looked . . . Strange, he was a man approaching his mid-years, and he had made love with at least a dozen women in his life. But he was never as captivated by any of their genitalia as he was by Toni-Ann's . . . Thinking about it almost made his smile, but he didn't, even though he was acknowledging a truth . . .

"We have *Scorpion* on our sonar screen, Comrade Admiral," the sonar officer reported to Borodine, who stood close to the periscope well. A chunkily built man, he gave the impression of having enormous physical strength, which he did possess, but he also projected an even greater inner strength, which the men saw in the almost electric glitter in his black eyes.

"Signal them that we have them on our sonar, and give

them our range and speed . . . We will approach them using our UWIS."

"Aye, aye, Comrade Admiral," the *Kiev*'s captain answered.

Borodine moved closer to the control console.

"The *Scorpion* acknowledges our transmission, and says that it has lost the ability to control the temperature conditions inside the boat."

Borodine nodded. "What is the condition of their air?" he asked, then he said, "Belay that . . . Patch me directly into the *Scorpion*."

"Admiral Boxer here," the voice said.

"This is Igor . . . What condition is your air?" Borodine asked.

"Very close to red," Boxer answered.

"We will maneuver alongside, as close as we can get," Borodine said. "Then I will launch a mini-sub, and it will fire a Harpoon—do you remember the Harpoon missiles?"

"All too well," Boxer answered.

"This one will have an air hose attached . . . The mini-sub will return to the *Kiev*, where the end of the hose will be attached to an air pump . . . We'll have you breathing fresh air in a couple of hours."

"Igor, we only have a couple of hours left . . . The temperature is down to fifty degrees, and some of the men are beginning to hallucinate."

"We'll be there in time, I promise you that," Borodine said, then added, "Save your strength . . . See you soon, old friend." He switched off, and moved away from the radio bank to the control console, where the *Scorpion* was already coming into view.

"She's sitting on the edge of an abyss," the *Kiev*'s

captain said, as he pointed to the *Scorpion*'s image.

Borodine nodded. He knew exactly what was going through the captain's mind . . . If for some reason the *Scorpion* should slip off its perch, and they were connected to it by a series of air hoses, it might well take them down with it. But it was a risk that had to be taken; otherwise everyone in the *Scorpion* would soon be dead. "Bring us as close as you can, to her starboard side . . . That way if she moves, she'll move against us, and we might just stop her."

"But that puts us over the abyss," the captain answered.

"Yes," Borodine answered, indicating by the tone of his voice that the matter was not open for discussion.

"Aye, aye, Comrade Admiral," the captain answered.

Boxer was beginning to feel the effects of the contaminated air. He was dizzy and nauseated at the same time. He had great difficulty focusing his eyes on any one thing, or one person. And when he spoke, he couldn't hear what he said. It seemed to him that he somehow managed to visit his old neighborhood again, and climb the back of the billboard to play pirate ship, and—

"Admiral—"

The voice was close.

"Admiral—"

Boxer swiveled his head toward the sound, and forced his eyes to focus.

"Admiral—"

"Oh, Sonny, I didn't know you were here," Boxer said, or at least thought he said it . . . Sonny was his best friend, his very best friend.

"Admiral—"

"Sonny, I don't want to be an admiral . . . I want to be a captain . . . Have my ship, and—"

The boom of a sudden explosion stopped Boxer. He looked up toward the sail, where it took place.

"Admiral—"

Something fell across him.

"Sonny?" Boxer questioned. "Sonny?"

"No response, Comrade Admiral," the COMMO said.

Borodine checked the UWIS. The mini-sub was on its way back, unwinding a three-quarter-inch air hose behind it. "Start pumping air as soon as the hose is connected to the air pump."

"Aye, aye, Comrade Admiral," the *Kiev*'s captain responded.

"We already might be too late," Borodine growled.

Boxer felt as if his head would burst. The pain was so intense that it seemed the only wayto end the pain was to punish it by banging his head against the wall . . . A pain to end a pain! But to do even that he required energy that he didn't have. . . .

Then he heard the hissing sound; at first he was sure it was a snake, a large one . . . Then, as the pain in his head decreased, and his brain seemed to come alive again, Boxer managed a smile. He knew he was alive. He closed his eyes, and took several deep breaths. The air was sweet and clean. . . .